A TRAVELER'S TALE
A NOVEL

BY THE SAME AUTHOR

Istanbul to Montréal–the story of an immigrant, novel.
Crete on the Half Shell, memoir.
Love in the Age of Confusion, novel.

BYRON AYANOGLU

A TRAVELER'S TALE
A MEMOIR OF SORTS: LIFE ON THE ROAD

LIVRES
DC
BOOKS

Cover illustration by Stéphane Jorisch.
Author photograph by Algis Kemezys.
Book designed and typeset by Primeau Barey, Montreal.

Library and Archives Canada Cataloguing in Publication
Ayanoglu, Byron, author
A traveler's tale: a memoir of sorts : life on the road/Byron Ayanoglu.
Issued in print and electronic formats.
ISBN 978-1-897190-93-7 (bound).–ISBN 978-1-897190-92-0 (pbk.).–
ISBN 978-1-927599-18-1 (pdf).–ISBN 978-1-927599-19-8 (html)
1. Title.
PS8551.Y35T73 2013   C813'.6   C2013-905532-0
                                 C2013-905533-9

For our publishing activities, DC Books gratefully acknowledges the financial
support of the Canada Council for the Arts, of SODEC, and of the Government
of Canada through Canadian Heritage and the Canada Book Fund.

 Canada Council **Conseil des Arts**
for the Arts **du Canada**

Société
de développement
des entreprises
culturelles
Québec 🔳🔳
🔳🔳

Printed and bound in Canada.
Interior pages printed on FSC® certified environmentally responsible paper.
Distributed by Fitzhenry and Whiteside.

MIX
Paper from
responsible sources
FSC
www.fsc.org   FSC® C103114

DC Books
PO Box 666, Station Saint-Laurent
Montreal, Quebec H4L 4V9
www.dcbooks.ca

For Algis Kemezys,
my best friend and life-partner

and great thanks to:
Angela Leuck
Philippe Barey
Steve Luxton
Keith Henderson
Marc Glassman
Marion Lewis
Jack Blum

A TRAVELER'S TALE

Life away from home.
All is strange, no compass to guide me,
no landmarks, no recognizable frontiers.
Curious, potentially cruel, decidedly deceptive.
But, I can't go back, that much is clear.
The trick is to adapt.
The rest is easy.

PART I
JEFFERSON COOPER

CHAPTER ONE

In the beginning, if you're lucky, you're born in a hospital with antiseptics and a seasoned obstetrician; and if cursed, you die in another ward of the same hospital, where death reeks of useless drugs and your murky piss drains out through tubes as, slowly, all your systems disengage one by one, cutting off your hope, your sound, your light and finally your air.

It's what comes in-between that matters. The all too-few decades they call *life,* which for many are simply an over-long wait for death; for the rest an all too-short spell of eating-fucking-thinking-creating, and, one shocking day, dying unprepared.

It is among those privileged "others" that I can count myself, and it is of such a *life,* that I must now concede, I am a victim.

I say *victim,* because I don't remember why I did what I have done in the past nor have the vaguest notion of what I must do now to survive.

CHAPTER TWO

I suddenly woke up fully dressed and crumpled after a long sleep. It must have been a long sleep, a dreamless sleep, because I could remember nothing that had transpired before that morning.

I was in a small house in what turned out to be Bitez, the inland village of a seaside resort on the southwestern edge of Turkey, overlooking the southeastern coast of the Aegean. I found out all these details later, by looking at a map. I had no idea what I was doing there–it was midwinter, cold and rainy, so I couldn't have been on holiday–nor how I had gotten there.

There was a man who seemed to be in charge of the place, a compact holiday-village, six two-story cottages around a garden with mandarin-orange trees. He told me in American English that I had arrived the previous night, late, way after midnight, and he had let me in even though the place was closed in the off-season, I looked so miserable that he took pity on me. I remembered none of this. In fact, I had no idea where I had come from and, most perplexingly, who I was.

I rummaged through my bag and my pockets, but I found nothing. No wallet. No passport.

"Oh, I have your passport," he said.

"Can I have it back?" I asked.

"Sure," he said, "soon as I can find it."

"It's very important to me," I mumbled.

"Of course it is," he shrugged. "It's your passport."

"It's more than just that," I started and hesitated.

"Yes...." he urged me in a mellow voice and earnest concern in his eyes.

"I don't know who I am," I blurted. "I seem to have forgotten everything. Even my name."

"Really?" he asked, suddenly preoccupied. "That must be terrible. Terrible. You have all my sympathy. I'll make you a wonderful Turkish breakfast. You'll feel better, I promise." He turned to leave.

"Please find my passport," I urged.

He retreated into his office and shut the door. I pinched myself to make sure I wasn't still sleeping and this was all some bizarre dream I was having somewhere in another country where I was someone with a history and a name and a wallet and a passport.

The man returned, "My name is Ahmet, and I lived a long time in New Jersey–too long," he said, as he set down my breakfast. A crusty pie of some kind, with a salty cheese filling. It was warm from his frying pan and tasty. I ate it in a hurry, I was frightfully hungry, as if I hadn't eaten for a long time. What about my passport? I asked him in-between mouthfuls, and he gave me tea, like a palliative, telling me that something silly must have happened, my passport appeared to have gotten lost. He hadn't yet written down any of its details, like my name, or what country it was from, but he remembered, from a cursory perusal, that I was thirty-three years old. I said that I hoped he was joking, but no he said, he was not. I was thirty-three, and my passport was lost, but not to worry, where could it have gone, I had given it to him just last night, and there wasn't another soul in the place. Could someone have stolen it? I asked. And why should anyone do that? he scoffed. He was a handsome man, around sixty years-old, and a bit too smug, too articulate for my liking.

After that he left me alone, and I continued to look through my bag, frantic. Not because I had no idea who I was or why I was there, or even that I was so obviously in a foreign country and my passport had gone missing, but very definitely because I seemed to have no money, and this was a cause of great concern. I might have forgotten all else, but I most decidedly remembered that without money you're a dead duck. I practically tore the bag apart. I was feeling desperate, angry, panicked and I finally threw it against the wall. It bounced off and hit the marble floor with such force that its bottom cracked open, and a plastic bag half-popped out of some secret compartment I had no idea was there. I pulled out the bag and looked inside. It was tightly stuffed with ten bundles of hundred-dollar bills, each secured with an elastic band. I was too shocked to do much more than stare at the bundles for what seemed an eternity. My shock turned to giddy relief, and I quickly counted the money. There were exactly ten thousand dollars in each bundle, which made one hundred thousand dollars in all.

A fortune at any time, and a particular solace for my predicament of the moment. On the other hand a real hazard, so much money in cash. I took out some few thousand and stuffed it into my pants pocket. I replaced the rest into the plastic bag and fitted it back into the false bottom of the suitcase. Miraculously the latch had only come apart and not broken as I feared. I pressed on it and the bag resealed seamlessly. It was now hidden from immediate view, but I knew that I would always have to fret and keep my eye fixed on the bag. If the bag were to be stolen, so would my newfound security. I removed the bag to the safety of the little bedroom upstairs.

The money back in its cache, it raised all manner of questions to further cloud my mind. Where did it come from? and why was I carrying so much cash in these days of bank machines and credit cards? Was I a thief, a smuggler, some kind of government operative like in the movies? Was I on the run? An eccentric millionaire?

It occurred to me that not only did I not know who I was, where I had come from, and why there was such a large bundle of cash in the secret pocket of my suitcase, but also that I had no mental image of what I looked like. I wearily walked into the bathroom.

A stranger looked back at me from the mirror. Not too terrible a sight, I mused. Tired and scruffy, yes, with bags under the eyes and sallow skin, but youthful under all that, attractive, almost. Short-cropped brown hair with blond highlights (dyed?), proportioned features–an artist's rendering could easily adjust my face to the golden ratio of 1:1.618–a nice nose, neither too big nor too small, full lips, high cheekbones, a slightly weak chin–that is where a painter or a good photographer could come handy to fortify–and remarkable eyes of a very unusual blue-grey colour. A normal body, tending to softness but far from flabby, and very toned arms and legs, as if I had been involved in some kind of sport. Out of curiosity I undressed to check out my crotch and discovered that there too nature had been generous with a plentiful penis that could appeal to either women or men, if only I had a clue as to my orientation, if any. For now, the situation appeared stable and limp, and I supposed, open to suggestion. Also to a wash. There were ripe smells wafting up to my nose. I showered, and put on some fresh clothes.

There was a knock on the door and I opened it to find Ahmet, grinning sheepishly. My passport must have indeed disappeared, he said. Now that he had given it some thought, he claimed I never actually handed it over to him. I showed it to him briefly and took it back, and that is why he hadn't had time to imprint any details outside of my birthdate and why he couldn't find it. I was certain he was lying, but I had no recourse. Not to worry, he said. If I had any money, a couple of thousand dollars, he knew someone, who knew someone, who could get me a new passport, even today. He stole a shy glance at me, arousing my suspicion that he already knew of my secret stash. Let's keep looking for your passport, he said, and if it's truly lost, we can talk. Two thousand is rather a lot and I don't know if I could find so much money in such a hurry, I said. Not too convincingly, I guess, because he smiled cunningly and left me.

CHAPTER THREE

My fake passport arrived within the hour. A Canadian document, well-used, with a half-spent multiple-entry Turkish visa on an inside page, and an equally half-spent, multiple-entry Indian visa on another, made out to Jefferson Cooper (a silly name, but better than none), aged thirty-three, born in Wawa, Ontario (where the heck is that? I would have refused to be born there), currently living in Montreal. Mr. J. Cooper's photo had been carefully removed from its designated space. Ahmet's friend, the passport "expert" Ali reached into his satchel and brought out a camera and a portable printer. He posed me in front of a white wall (all walls in Bitez seemed to be white) warning me not to smile (apparently Canadians do not normally smile). He then deftly pasted the picture onto the page, stamped it with authority and covered it neatly with clear plastic.

He handed me my new identity, smugly pleased with himself, and looked meaningfully at my hands. I gave him my pre-counted two thousand dollars, which he leafed crisply and looked at Ahmet askance. Ahmet smiled at me mischievously taking the two grand from Ali's hand. "My fee for helping you is two thousand, my friend," he said imperiously. "Ali's fee for the service is four thousand, and cheap at the price." I was obviously being had, but what choice did I have? I excused myself into my bedroom, and struggled with my suitcase until I got its secret compartment open, and came back with the money.

CHAPTER FOUR

I packed quickly and quit the premises soon after Ali had departed with a big smile on his face and my four grand in his pocket, and before Ahmet could concoct new ways to extort more money from me. I went into a store and asked to buy cigarettes (apparently I was a smoker). The clerk didn't bat an eyelash when I offered to pay him with a hundred-dollar bill, giving me a mess of Turkish Liras in change.

A little bus that had fortuitously arrived as soon as I was back on the street took me ten kilometres east into Bodrum's central bus station, where I sat down to have a glass of stewed tea and assess my situation.

I appeared to be displaying all the classic symptoms of selective amnesia: I was cognizant of the ways of the world and still master of language and accepted behaviour; I could reason and function; I could recall societal, historical, geographical common-knowledge, even trivial facts, some science (whatever I must have learned and picked up in my original state), and arithmetic and even more complicated mathematics and details of books that I must have read and movies that I must have watched, and all manner of other captured knowledge, and yet I couldn't for the life of me remember a single incident of my own experiences, not an iota of my personal history!

Was it amnesia, or simply a refusal to remember? Had my life been so traumatic (or so very boring) that I had blocked it all out in favour of a clean slate? Now that I was over the initial panic of absolute darkness about my past, I found some solace in a predicament that opened a sea of possibilities. It made me happy that I was now free to start a brand new life, one filled with travel to visit places I might have already seen and many that I surely had never seen or even heard about during my murky, indecipherable first life. Now, it was time to board the bus that would take me away to wherever I didn't know I had always wanted to go.

CHAPTER FIVE

An overlong rumination about my condition, sitting at the rickety table of the bus station's cafe with seven glasses of crimson tea and three regulation waiting-room sandwiches came to a merciful halt when a distinguished, older man sat beside me uninvited. He introduced himself as Özdemir, a poet named after another famous Turkish poet, and instantly found out that I had no destination in mind, even though I was sitting at a bus station clutching a suitcase.

"Istanbul is the most logical place on which to alight from any point in Turkey," he said in Oxford-tinted, purposefully well-spoken English. "It is the largest and historically our most significant city. It is the cultural hub of a nation whose language is shared by no one else even in its own region. Therefore its hegemony over our destiny is supreme and comprehensive. If anything memorable is happening in Turkey, it's bound to be in Istanbul. It is a city that throughout its fifteen-hundred year chronicle has been known simply as the City. More Eternal even than Rome, this Seat of the Greek Orthodox Church, resisted all adversity to remain a capital and nerve center of two successive empires for fifteen hundred years and to reign today as the definitive geopolitical link between Europe and Asia, the New World and the Old, Christianity and Islam. It is both the entry and exit point for anywhere else domestic or foreign that one is headed, and the bus destination most faithfully served from anywhere in the country, including Bodrum"

He stroked his greying beard and patted his thinning ponytail before continuing his hype on Istanbul with some serious name dropping: "It is a city of luminaries. Constantine, his mother Helen, Julian the Apostate, Baudolino, Fatih its Conqueror, Suleiman the Magnificent who came very close to conquering all of Europe,

Atatürk the founder of our Republic, Agatha Christie, Mata Hari, James Bond... oh so many," he mused, concluding his rap with a suggestion (a directive?) that I board the bus right across the tea-terrace in exactly half an hour, and "Here's fifty Turkish Lira for the ticket," thinking me to be broke, I guess, considering I was at a bus station with nowhere to go. Then he had excused himself to go fetch cigarettes and disappeared.

I did try to wait for him to return and at least give him back his money since I had so much of it already. After twenty-five minutes, and without particularly meaning to, I walked across the tarmac, bought a ticket with forty-five of his fifty Liras and boarded the evening bus to the City, obligated to concede my suitcase to the hold since it was too big to take inside and I had totally neglected to transfer the money into a more manageable bag.

The ride was long and uneventful. I slept through most of it and only opened my eyes when the engine gave out a loud sigh before going silent to signify the definitive end of the journey. We had arrived at a bus depot in some desolate part of town where Suleiman the Magnificent wouldn't have wasted even a minute during his continent-rousing mission. Seemingly-untampered suitcase in hand I was herded into a smaller bus that rattled across terminally traffic-congested roads until it reached Taksim, the heart of the modern city. It was drizzling, cold, dark, not in the least welcoming.

I walked across the crowded square, almost trampled by a flock of swirling pigeons, feeling the burden of the suitcase more with every step. To my right was a frilly road with an ancient tramcar its only vehicle and a tsunami of pedestrians moving in both directions. There were several hotels with luxurious façades to my left. I applied to three of them in a row, only to be refused check-in because I lacked a credit card, despite my willingness to prepay the room in American cash. The receptionist of the third one, as haughty as his colleagues in the first two, turned out to be a nice guy and told me to walk down one block on Istiklal Caddesi (the walking-street with the tramcar), turn left and try one of the less demanding hotels down there.

I struggled through the thick people-traffic of Istiklal dwarfed on both sides by its contiguous string of flashy storefronts with window displays alternating between fashion and food. Already cold, wet and disoriented, I was devastated when a seductive brunette in the glory of her early forties, well-dressed in svelte shades of black, furiously confronted me and slapped me hard across the face.

"You bastard!" she yelled in Spanish as she side-swept me to meld into the crowd and out of my view. My cheek was burning and my eyes started to water.

CHAPTER SIX

She was obviously a mistake of my past, some unforgivable sin of mine having scarred her to the quick, an affront for which I could repent and relentlessly regret if I only knew what it was. It occurred to me to delve into the crowd and try to find her, to appease her, but the mere thought of it made me nauseous. The suitcase had by now become a bitter cross to bear, and my cheek, which she had ripped with her ring, was stinging; but much more than the physical discomfort, I was aching with a sadness that overwhelmed me. The walkers seemed to have picked up speed, running right at me from all directions at once, as if they meant to tackle me to the ground. The store lights throbbed with urgency, blinding me. A shiver went through me, and then tears, tears. A desolate, unhappy outburst, a wet consequence of my unbearable predicament. Purely by instinct I sidled over to the side of the road, and exhausted I slid to the ground, curled around my suitcase, buried my head in my arms, and sobbed.

I felt a soft hand gently touching my shoulder. I looked up and saw her through my veil of tears. She was smiling, I think, kindly. She was thin and ethereal in a weather-defying lightweight turquoise dress and delicate golden sandals. She had a red, tulip-shaped hat atop lime-coloured tresses that fell to her neck in waves. Her face was moonshine, silver and bright, she could have been sixteen or sixty. She dried my tears with a silk handkerchief, helped me up, and led me into a cafe away from the chaos of the street.

"My name is Miryam," she said in Turkish. "It is the same as Mary." It didn't surprise me that I understood her language. It was becoming obvious that I should allow nothing to ever surprise me again.

"My name is… Cooper," I said, not being able to say "Jeff," let alone "Jefferson."

"Okay, Cooper. Now, drink your tea, it'll help you to forget her," she winked.

A curvy glass of blood-red tea had magically materialized in front of me, courtesy of an extra-discreet waiter. I took a gulp that almost burned my throat, but as she said, it soothed me. She wet the edge of a napkin from tea in her own glass and wiped the blood off the cut on my cheek with a light touch.

"What would really cheer you up," she said with a twinkle in the eye, "is some dancing. I always dance when I'm depressed."

"Dancing? At this hour of the morning?"

"I know a place that swings twenty-four hours a day."

"But, but, my suitcase!"

"We'll leave it at the coat-check." She perceived my discomfort. "What have you got in there? Piles of money?"

"No-o," I lied. "But, I was trying to find a hotel."

"Fine. Be boring. Let's find you a hotel." And she led me out of the cafe after throwing some coins on the table.

She walked me to a clean looking, but modest and probably unsafe place and helped me to secure a room. She kissed me wetly on the healthy cheek. "I'll come back for you in a few hours. Be here!" And she exited with one last, alluring glance amid a fragrant trace of jasmine & musk.

Finally behind a locked door, I looked around for a place to hide my money. I decided against piling all of it in one nook. I divided it into four lots, squeezing each one into a different part of the ceiling behind tiles that came undone when pushed inward, marking the locations with barely visible "x's" with the ballpoint I found on the little desk. I took note of their distance from the corners of the ceiling, praying that I would be able to find them all again.

I really did want to see that little Miryam, to dance with her, and hopefully to have sex, all of which activities I felt sure I could perform by tapping into resources I couldn't articulate but must in some fashion have possessed. She had said "a few hours," but I felt too tired to stay awake waiting for her. I lay back on the lumpy bed to make the time pass and must have fallen into a deep sleep, because all I remembered when I woke up many hours later, some-time in the twilight of late afternoon, was a remote but insistent ring of the house phone which I had registered as part of a dream where bells were summoning me but I was too scared to respond. It was raining in earnest outside and a wintry wind was noisily filtering down my narrow street. I would have liked her company. Instead I had to face the evening alone.

CHAPTER SEVEN

I took one last look at all four of my money caches, trying to imprint them since the ballpoint "x's" were faint, and I left the room to walk out into the cold wetness. I swung to the right at the top of the street to head down Istiklal, which spat out shards of light into the drab night. Despite the insistent, near-frigid rain it had become even more crowded and frenetic as the citizens searched for adventure with which to overcome the wintry conditions.

I changed some dollars for Turkish Liras and looked around. Food beckoned from every nook. There were mounds of darkly shiny mussels on street-vendors' stalls next to charred chestnuts on the glowing embers of another itinerant. In windows, rows of crusted sweets glowed golden-brown, while meats on skewers sizzled on coal-fires. Appetizing, distantly familiar smells wafted. I hadn't eaten since yesterday at the bus depot. I chose a place at random, mostly because it was crowded, and sat down at a table for two.

A man of about my age entered mere seconds after me. He had darting eyes and a strange haircut, spiky like a pineapple, so black it had to be dyed. He came over and sat at my table. "Hello," he said with some urgency.

"Do you know me?" I asked, daring to hope he could tell me about myself.

"Know you!" he exclaimed with unnecessary force. "How the hell am I supposed to know you?"

"Well... well," I stammered, "you sat at my table. You said 'hello,' I thought...."

"That's probably your biggest problem. You think too much. You think you're important. Well, you're not! You're nobody. Just like me. We are one of a kind, you and me. We are two nobodies, and this meeting hasn't really happened. I can get up and leave, you know. I can just disappear, if you'd rather sit here all alone."

"I don't give a damn what you do," I snapped, although I wanted him to stay. He had somehow figured me out in a flash. I was a *nobody*, far as I knew.

"On the other hand, I'd like very much to eat with you, but I'm sorry. I have no money," he conceded, lowering his eyes.

"That's okay with me," I said.

We sat for a while, not looking at each other. Suddenly he turned very serious and peered at me. "I am not from here," he said in Arabic. "I don't expect you to understand me, but then again, no one understands me," he smiled.

"I understand totally," I replied in Arabic, smiling but in a melancholy way.

"Are you Arab," he asked.

"No, I am not," I said, "not as far as I know."

The waiter approached us at that point, obviating explanations. My newfound friend ordered for both of us in rapid-fire Turkish which I could not make out. "You chose an excellent restaurant," he nodded. "I come here all the time. They know me here. They treat me well. Very well."

"You said you had no money," I poked.

"Oh, I have money. Lots of money. I was testing you. I have so much money, that I will be paying for you. You watch. I am a very tricky person. I was testing you, but don't worry. You passed. That's why I haven't left. That's why I'm still sitting here, and why I will be eating with you. I don't eat with just anybody, you know, and it's also why I'll be paying for you. Okay?"

"Yeah, yeah, okay." That last speech had annoyed me.

"Aren't you happy that I'll be paying for you?" he asked playfully.

"You don't have to pay for me. I was ready to pay for you," I reminded him.

"I know that! That's why I'll pay. I insist. No one likes to pay for people who have no money. That's a fact! It's my treat. I want to pay for you, because I want to stay and talk to you. I have a secret I want to tell you, but first I must get to know you better." He had slipped back into English. He was beginning to confuse me. I was starting to wish he would leave me alone, but it was too late. The first course he had ordered was on the table. A plate of shredded meats with what looked suspiciously like a pair of eyes in the middle.

"It's a sheep's head," he announced proudly. "In the old days they used to serve it simply chopped in half and you had to dig the eyes out of the sockets with your fingers, but now they take it apart and throw away the bones. The jaw bones with the tiny yellowed teeth are particularly offensive. It's much more civilized this way, don't you think?"

"I hate it," I said petulantly. "I don't want to even look at it."

"That's because it's looking at you," he said with a guffaw. "I hate it, too. I was testing you, silly!" He summoned the waiter with impatient finger-snapping and told him gruffly to take it away. The waiter promptly replaced it with a plate of fried calamari and a lively salad of wild greens. "Now, isn't that better?" he asked proudly.

"Yes, it is," I said, digging in. The calamari was crisp on the outside and creamy-soft on the inside. The salad was bitter and sweet all at once. He added some thick vinegar, "sour of pomegranate" he called it, that made it even better. We ate quickly with no wasted words.

"See, we're getting to know each other in a great hurry," he mumbled between mouthfuls.

We exchanged names. I told him I was Cooper, once again refusing to mention "Jefferson"; he said he was Hussein. "Like Saddam," he added wistfully. "And I am from Iraq. Also like Saddam."

"Is that where we met?" I asked him, trying to trick him.

"We've never met anywhere," he answered me with finality. The waiter swept away our spent appetizer plates and immediately replaced them with heaping portions of grilled lamb-kebabs on rice pilaf, singed hot peppers and roasted half-tomatoes on the side. Again we gorged in silence.

"Do you want dessert?" he hinted.

"I'm too full, thanks," I said, listlessly, as if wishing him to get up and leave.

"Do you want me to leave?" he asked, reading my mind if not my body language.

"You can stay, if you like," I replied cheerlessly.

"If I leave, you'll have to pay," he threatened.

"I don't mind," I shrugged.

"And you don't care about my secret that I promised you?"

"What secret?"

"Exactly, as I thought. You don't care about anyone but yourself," he complained matter-of-factly.

"That's not really true," I countered. "It's just that I forgot what you said."

"Exactly!"

"I was too hungry. I was only thinking about—"

"—your stomach!"

"And what's wrong with that?"

"Nothing, I guess. But you're missing out on a good secret, that's all."

"Okay, I bite. What's your secret?" I tried to sound disinterested.

"You don't give a fuck for my secret. Admit it."

"You have no cause to swear at me," I said, self-righteously. "I never asked you for any secret. I didn't even know you had a secret."

"Exactly!"

"What 'exactly'? Exactly what?" I was getting annoyed, and by now I really did want him to leave me alone.

"Well, since you ask: I am not who you think I am. And I didn't just sit here by chance. I happen to know you and all about what you did!"

"Aha!" I exclaimed a bit too loudly. "So tell me," trying to sound much less excited than I felt. "Go on, I'm listening."

"Right. Exactly. Now, he's listening." He paused meaningfully. "As I said, you're only interested in yourself, but it's not going to be free. You'll have to buy me a dessert. Then, I'll tell you everything."

"Oh, you're impossible," I waved my hand. "Fine, order anything you want. Eat it, enjoy it, and tell me whatever it is you know; or don't, it doesn't much matter to me!"

"Of course it matters," he winked. "You'll see!"

He snapped his fingers for the waiter, and then he froze. There were two policemen watching the restaurant from the rain outside. "I'll be right back," he said in Arabic, and casually hid his face with his hand as he stood up. He walked quickly to the rear of the restaurant, and out the fire exit. I chuckled at his con-game, considering myself the winner since he had unwittingly provided me with highly dubious but entertaining dinner companionship.

I noticed a little slip of paper on his side of the table. I scooped it up as casually as I could, though my heart was racing. Its message was yet another slap on my face: "You're no Jefferson, Mr. Cooper. And no amount of names'll save you."

CHAPTER EIGHT

I sprang out of my seat and rushed out the fire exit to find him. It was a dark alley in a maze of alleys, rain-shiny in shades of slimy black. It smelled of garbage. There were some dishwasher types outside neighbouring restaurant back doors smoking cigarettes which they were cupping in their palms to keep dry. He was nowhere in sight.

I knew it would be useless to go darting off into the labyrinth to look for him. I returned into the warmth of the restaurant, happy that the fire exit hadn't locked shut behind me. The waiter with my bill in hand was already talking to the policemen on the street. I walked up to him apologetically and squeezed two hundred-Lira bills into his hand, mumbling, "Keep the change," in Turkish. I turned away regretting my largesse which could well have been misinterpreted by the police.

Too late to repair the damage, I walked away casually so as not to elicit further suspicion, mercifully being quickly engulfed by the throng of walkers which appeared to have substantially increased in the last hour. I let their momentum carry me down the street past the ornate Belle Epoque architecture and the relentless merchandising of the unending strip of shop-fronts.

At its halfway point, the street widened into a plaza with the filigreed wrought iron gates of a private high school on one side and the entrance to an outdoor fish-market on the other. This seemed to be a crossover point for the walkers, who circled the plaza as if uncertain which way to continue pursuing their peripatetic aimlessness, until a wave could take shape and the inexhaustible, snake-paced parade could slither back to its path. I squeezed my way out of the flow and landed at an outdoor table of a crowded cafe. It had an awning to ward off the rain and outdoor heaters to soften the cold.

"You must order the Mexican hot chocolate," said a female voice from the adjacent table. "It's their specialty and the only item worth what they charge." I turned to face a buxom older woman who appeared to be dressed entirely in several layers of multicoloured scarves which were loosely tied over her entire body, from her head to her legs. "I love scarves," she added as if I couldn't see that for myself.

I should have by now been primed that someone or other would befriend me (or slap me or berate me) uninvited, but she startled me nevertheless. "Don't worry, I'm harmless," she said in her own defense. "It's just that you seem so confused, I thought I would put you at ease."

"I will order the chocolate," I conceded. "Thank you."

"Isn't it funny how we Istanbullus are so determined to sit outside even in this devilish weather," she continued. "It's the damned smoking laws. We can only do it outside." And she lit up a Gauloise, which prompted me to realize she was speaking French.

"Are you from France?"

"Not at all," she shook her head vehemently. "I am from here, but I've lived in Montreal." She took a deep drag on her cigarette, filling the air with toasty smoke. "Like yourself," she added.

"How did you know I'm from Montreal?"

I might have become really apprehensive, if I had half a mind to do so. I was from no particular place that I could name, but it did say I lived in Montreal in the fake passport I had bought in Bitez.

"I have a nose for such things," she winked. "As you know, I am a travel agent."

"Then you could probably help me," I said absorbing the "as you know" as part of her sales pitch, while at the same time ordering a Mexican hot chocolate from the harried waiter who had finally found time to come to my table.

"Where would you like to go?"

"I don't know," I said with total sincerity.

"Then I know exactly the place for you," she beamed.

"Well, that's wonderful," I said.

She peered at me for a few seconds, then reached into her bag and brought out a folder. "I have only one word for you," she said weightily, and then paused dramatically. I waited patiently for her to continue and dazzle me with her singular word. My hot chocolate arrived. It was indeed wonderful, thick and dark with hints of cinnamon and chilies. I took a big gulp and swirled it in my mouth. It warmed me down to my toes. She smiled at my palpable satisfaction, pleased that her suggestion was being appreciated, and finally let me know her "one word": *Cambodia!* she announced triumphantly, pronouncing it in a quasi French version as "Cambogj-ya."

"I see," I mumbled halfheartedly.

"You know, I am nude underneath the scarves," she admitted. "If someone were to pull them off me I'd be quite embarrassed," giggling as if she were daring me to do so.

"Also frozen," I winked, giggling right back at her cold-heartedly.

"Cambodg is the newest 'discovery' of discerning travelers," she continued, opening her folder to luscious tropical images. "It has better beaches than Thailand, better food than Viet Nam, excellent accommodation and service at next to no cost, and hasn't quite become the bordello that Thailand has turned into, while at the same time, being equally Buddhist as Thailand, it offers all the same amenities, if you get my drift," and she winked again.

"And I suppose you could sell me a ticket to *Cambodg* right here where we are sitting," I suggested, pre-empting her obvious next pitch.

"As a matter of fact, I can," she answered, ignoring my sarcasm and reaching again into her bag to bring out a book of vouchers and a small credit card machine. "Three hundred American, one way, direct Istanbul-Mumbai, with a short hop from there to Phnom Penh, all inclusive, and I'll throw in the bus to the airport, a visa valid for one month, which you can renew endlessly, and two nights in a four-star in the best quarter of the capital. Really, it's the best place for you right now."

"That's awfully nice," I chuckled demurely, sipping some more of the restorative chocolate. "But, now that you've mentioned it, Bombay would be more my cup of tea." I said, thinking I was teasing her, but sensing some deeply buried attachment to that renamed Indian metropolis.

"Listen," she drew herself closer to me for emphasis. "You're not ready for Mumbai. That city is a cauldron of conflicting emotions. A maze from which you may never again emerge. A hellhole that is dressed in fine silks with which to seduce you before she delivers the *coup de grâce* right into your heart. Anyway, you were there recently and barely managed to escape. Why push your luck. Go and relax in Cambodia. In any case I can't get you a visa for India on such short notice." She had switched to elegantly pronounced English.

"I have a valid Indian visa," I remarked, remembering it from a quick inspection of J. Cooper's passport that was now my only identity.

"Of course you do. I should have known that. But, why on earth would you want to return to that incredibly disheveled place? It'll only boggle your mind more than it already is." She sidled even closer to me, almost touching me.

"That's exactly what I do want," I countered just to be contrary, or maybe because my secret real self did have a valid reason to go there; it didn't matter. I drew a little back from her proximity, which emanated a lived-in odour of piss and stale perfume. "I need to be challenged. I have no desire to 'relax.' On the contrary."

"Bombay it is then. It is a beautiful city, full of wonder and delight," she said brightly, moving back to her original distance. "Four hundred and fifty return, bus to the airport, and a complimentary afternoon-tea at the Taj Hotel, the moment they reopen it. Best I can do and a very good deal at that. Plane leaves at ten a.m. You give me fifty dollars now, then I come to your hotel early in the morning and take you to the airport myself. You pay the balance at the airport as you check in. Fair?"

"Will you take cash?" I asked as I finished off the chocolate.

"I love cash," she laughed as she grabbed my money and handed me a receipt and her card.

"It's a deal, then," I smiled reading her name on the card, "and thank you for your help... Aishe."

CHAPTER NINE

I bought a carry-on bag and a leatherette wallet from an outdoor stall on my way back to the hotel. I didn't quite know why I had so readily agreed to the trip in the morning, but like everything else in the last day and a half the opportunity had come knocking on my door of its own accord and I could think of no good reason to refuse it. At worst it meant losing fifty dollars if she were to turn out to be a fake.

All of my money was where I had left it in the various hiding places of my hotel room's ceiling. I retrieved the lot and sat on my bed fondling it. I somehow felt certain that at one point of this improbable journey it would be lost or stolen from me. But, it sure was comforting while I still had it.

I rammed as much as could fit into my new wallet and piled the rest of the large wads into the carry-on. I repacked my clothes, which I noticed for the first time were mostly lightweight summer-wear. It made me wonder which tropical location I had last vis-ited (lived in?) before I ended up on the Aegean coast of Turkey. Unwieldy mysteries weighing on my mind, I lay back on the much-used, cheap mattress and settled into a half-awake dream of a pon-derous walk through a thorny-unfriendly garden, danger lurking behind every ominous bush.

Exhausted, I got out of bed just as a hazy dawn was reluctantly colouring the sky grey. The rain had stopped, but the cloud cover held its darkening grip over the City, a primal cause of its inhabit-ants' collective melancholy, their *hüzün,* so evocatively described by Orhan Pamuk.

I packed my belongings and went down to breakfast to wait for Aishe. There was no one else there at this early hour and the badly lit breakfast room looked even larger than it was for the size of the hotel. A waiter emerged from the shadows, bearing an uncomfortably toothy smile. He came very close to me and ceremoniously spread a huge, stiffly ironed, cloth napkin on my lap.

"Coffee, tea, anything you want," he pronounced it "vant" and continued breathlessly, "Turkish breakfast, olives, *tahin-petmez, simit, bogatsa,* toast-bread of all kind, cheeses, salamis, everything on buffet, all you want, I know you love our breakfast last visit you stay, other tourist say they come to Istanbul just to have our breakfast, all you want, and until twelve o'clock in the noontime, no hurry, you can eat here many hours, until you are full for the whole day, eggs, too, fried in the *hasan,* boiled, *à la coque,* anything you want, same like last month when you were here, also we make full English breakfast, but that's extra money, eggs, toast, beans, fried tomato, potato, mushrooms, and best of all, real pork bacon, real pork sausage, from England, it is very nice day, no rain today, only some cloud, so, what is it you want?" He finished his rehearsed speech with a smile even more crippling than the original.

"Just Turkish tea, please," I replied in Turkish without a hint of a reciprocal smile. "Did you say I was here last month?"

"Okay, okay, I bring tea," he said, palpably offended by my question, or maybe my lack of enthusiasm, and retreated into the shadows.

Aishe walked into the room and perused the emptiness, until she spotted me with a sigh of intense pleasure. "Aah, there you are," she chirped. "I was wondering if I would have to drag you out of bed!" She was dressed in a whole new set of scarves, one of which had come slightly undone revealing a bit more of her aging left breast than she would have liked to show.

The waiter brought two teas with a scornful glance my way, as if to say, "I'm a much better waiter than you deserve." We finished them in a hurry, and I left him a ten Lira tip to show him that I was a much better customer than he took me for. Aishe led the way to the airport bus, and chatted inanely the whole way without in the least needing me to respond. I thought I caught some mention of other times she had booked my flights, but she cascaded past it so smoothly I didn't get a chance to quiz her. At a given moment she must have readjusted the scarf around her torso, because I was spared any further peeks of her errant nipple.

She became all businesslike at the Air-India counter, booked me in, handed me the documents and motioned to my wallet. I paid her and she immediately turned around and left me with a hurried, *"Bon voyage et au revoir."*

CHAPTER TEN

Mumbai's Chhatrapati Shivaji International Airport is the most important gateway to the Subcontinent. It is as spiffy and modern as the best of them, but it is still India. Overcrowded, borderline chaotic, permanently congested and now further encumbered by what seemed an army of police with machine guns and growling sniffing-dogs. How anyone can find anyone coming out of it defies logic, and yet, there he was at the arrivals queue, a pleasant young man, cheerful if a little uncomfortable in his starched white shirt and tightly knotted, colourful tie, holding a placard with "Mr Jefferson Cooper" in crimson, carefully crafted lettering. Thinking, "Aah, that wily Aishe," I approached him and before I could introduce myself he smiled sunnily and spoke a tad too loudly:

"Mr. Cooper, sir, your car is ready outside and your room awaits you at the Yacht Club. It is my immense pleasure to assist you and may I take your bags?" He was obviously well-educated and far too qualified for this menial position.

"Oh, why not," giving him the suitcase but not my handbag. "I didn't know Aishe had connections like these in Mumbai."

"We're not acquainted with any Aishe, sir. The Club's president, Mr. Akhbar Singh personally sent me to fetch you." He bowed, taking my suitcase and leading the way to the car. "I'm Arvind, Mr. Singh's son," he said, as if apologizing.

"It's good to be someone's son," I assured him. "But how did Mr. Singh know I was coming today?" I asked, trying to sound only mildly interested.

"Your reservation, sir. You made it before you left last time you stayed with us. And you confirmed it last week by email, and again last night by fax that you were taking this flight. You must have forgotten. These long flights can really play havoc with one's mind."

"Yes, I guess they can," I replied uneasily. These people seemed to know more about me and my movements than I did. It was time to get some answers, and I surmised that this amiable fellow would be easy to drill. I was wrong.

"Do you remember what I was doing in Mumbai on my last visit?"

He seemed highly offended to hear my question. "Sir, I certainly do not," he scoffed. "And if I did, I certainly could not say! We never disclose the business of our guests to anyone."

"Even to themselves?"

"Especially to themselves," he protested, as if I was trying to trick him and catch him at an indiscretion. He helped me into the car, and brightened up once he was in the chauffeur's position with me in the back, even though it was not exactly a limousine, but rather a narrow Korean compact, with the distance between himself and me no more than a couple of feet. "There will be some traffic on the way, sir. We're having onion troubles and there is a major demonstration in Bundra that extends all the way to the exits of the highway."

He proceeded to bring me up to date with all the minutiae of the onion situation, an indispensable component of Indian cuisine, without which neither rich nor poor could possibly enjoy their meals, and the prices of which were going through the roof due to lack of regulation by an uncaring government and the greed of onion conglomerates who were creating a shortage by exporting the valuable bulb to neighbouring equally onion-dependent countries for extra profit.

Sure enough, not more than five kilometres from the airport we were at a virtual standstill, as crazed, onion-deprived gourmets of a city that was built on landfill by Brits who will only reluctantly eat onions with liver (if that), were screamingly tearing up and down the tarmac waving onion-shaped banners, daring the masses of police and soldiers to buck them.

I was too engrossed in the mayhem to notice her. A fluid beauty with torn rags and fiery, jet-black eyes had sidled right up to the back door of our Hyundai and without further ado yanked it open and thrust a bleeding handless stump at my face, wailing loudly with a beseeching tone that could melt an iceberg. There was fresh as well as caked blood on her wound, which must have recently been hacked with a dull knife by the looks of it.

I felt nauseous. I wanted to embrace her, to somehow make her egregious and insufferable injury bearable. I started reaching into my pocket to give her money, it was all I could think of doing stuck on a highway with no visible exit. Arvind was shouting from the driver's seat. At her in Hindi to get the hell out of the car and at me in English to push her out.

"Are you crazy?" I shouted back. "Look at what they did to her!"

"No one did anything to her!" he said icily, as he shoved the gear into neutral and jumped out to grab her and pull her away from me, as she screamed. "You look," he instructed patiently as he roughly yanked the bleeding stump off her wrist. A timid, perfectly unharmed hand emerged from her sleeve. He threw the grotesque prosthetic over the railing onto the crowd below the highway, and pushed her to the ground. She got up cursing him as she casually walked away. "They will stop at nothing to avoid honest work," he remarked as he climbed back into the driver's seat just in time to put the car in gear and take off at high speeds on the highway that had suddenly and magically been liberated and was back to functional.

The Royal Bombay Yacht Club, a High-Raj Victorian confection sits kitty-corner from another of the kind, the famous Taj Hotel. "We escaped unscathed at the Club, but the poor Taj is bandaged head to toe with scaffolding to repair the damage of the terrorist attacks," the younger Singh informed me while we waited to clear a police cordon before being allowed to drive into this most majestic corner of the city, right across from the Gate of India.

Mr. Ahkbar Singh himself greeted me in the front entrance and took the well-worn marble stairs two at a time backward as he led me up to my reserved room. I must have been a really good tipper in my former self. "It's always a great pleasure to greet the re-arrival of an esteemed seaman such as yourself, Mr. Cooper. As you know only esteemed seamen have the right to stay here, Commodores and higher. Admirals. Master Yachtsmen, such as yourself, and that's just about all."

The room to which he took me was more like an apartment, with a pantry off the entrance, a sizable bathroom with a shower as well as a bathtub where commodores and yachtsmen could de-grime after months at sea, a huge bedroom with a large sitting area, and the best up front, an executive office with a prime-ministerial desk and a wall of glass doors to an immense floral balcony that seemed perched right on top of the Gate and the endless seascape behind it.

Mr. Singh and his retinue of porters–all three of whom found a way to have a part in carrying my one suitcase, and all three of whom now needed to be tipped–retreated to become once again part of the Yacht Club's antiquated, long-lost, but highly appreci- ated ties to the British Empire, leaving me alone to blink several times to make sure it was all real.

I opened the balcony doors and stepped out into the liquid warmth of a Mumbai early morning. I sat on a cushioned metal chair, white and curlicued, straight out of a Cotswolds garden, and took in the view of an India from a hundred years ago, the only signifier of the current age a cacophony of traffic emanating from a street below that I couldn't see.

This was an ideal setting to take stock of self-regenerating events that, had I been so inclined, should be shocking me at every turn. A fortune in cash stashed into a suitcase, a passport that disappears and is promptly replaced, a ponytailed intellectual who instructs me to board a bus for Istanbul, a woman who slaps me and curses me on a crowded street, an elf who saves me, a suspect fellow who promises me a secret which turns out to be that he knew a fake first name I had never given him and which he declared was not my real name at all, an unsolicited travel agent who claimed to have previously served me and unceremoniously packed me off to India, where I was not only well-known, but had made a reservation to return to on the very day that I had unintentionally and entirely circumstantially did come (return?). The whole mess of inexplicable curiosities was exacerbated by the dizzying fact that I had no inkling of anything at all concerning my life prior to waking up in Bitez a mere three days ago.

I thought it best to abandon the quest and take instead a rest from the combined rigours of my incomprehension and the relentless traveling of the last seventy-two hours. I shut the balcony doors, drew the heavy curtains that cut off light and noise, took a shower, flicked on the air-conditioning and went to bed.

CHAPTER ELEVEN

I woke up around four in the afternoon hankering for an English-style tea, with thin sandwiches, little pastries and a bevy of wealthy little-old ladies, dressed to feel important, nibbling, sipping, gossiping on soft chairs. It was such a vivid picture that I had no doubt I must have indulged in it whether I remembered or not. I also had no doubt that there would be such a tea in this ever-so English place, and, yes, there it was only steps from my room down the corridor with its serial portraits of Commodores, Admirals and Master Yachtsmen, in the Tea Room (where else). The only variant, here the nibbling-sipping-gossipers were powerful old men.

I sat at an empty table for two and felt fairly certain that soon someone who knew me would be taking the other seat. I had turned away for a minute, to tell the waiter I wanted Lapsang with hot milk and no pastries but double on the sandwiches, and there he was. "Hi, Jeff," he said as he lowered himself gently onto the seat as if he was suffering from piles or was being careful not to unduly ruffle his freshly ironed, bespoke linen suit.

"Hello," I responded quizzically. He broke into a laugh. He was almost fifty with thick, elegantly greying hair, a seasoned face, an expensive get-up; the sort that you would expect to meet in a posh London casino, not a tea-room in a vestige of Old Bombay. "How silly of me to think you'd remember someone as humble as myself," he sighed and waved his hand towards his chest. "I am Krishna. We met in Delhi at, I must admit, a rather dull event."

"Sorry. It was a while back…." I bluffed.

"Oh, please, I'm not in the least offended. Just happy to be seeing you again, is all. We spoke at length, mostly about food," he hinted.

"Oh, yes, I think I remember," I lied.

"Actually, I promised you a brilliant Indian meal at the time, and this evening might just be the right moment to make good on it." He raised his eyebrows by way of asking me to dinner.

"It would give me great pleasure, I'm sure. But, tell me. What dull event were we attending in Delhi? I get so bored in that town I blank it out of my mind."

"An Indian meal is much like Indian music, Indian sunsets, or even, Indian romance," he intoned knowingly while totally ignoring my question. "It starts slowly, with mellow resonance and gentle stress. One or two flavours and some textural treats. It segues fairly soon into juicy, lusty, intensely colourful stews and grills and stir-fries that fire up the palate as they fuel the imagination and feed one's deepest and most secret desires. They become sheer pleasure, seemingly pure entertainment and quickly evaporate, should I say, levitate, as they survive to become irrepressible memories that in retrospect speak of the monumental meaning of the experience." He paused for effect, and to tell the waiter he was not going to have tea. "I must be off. Enjoy your tea. I'll fetch you at seven to take you to my humble palace for dinner. Yes?"

"I'll be ready," I said, and to prove I was sincere I stood up to shake his hand good-bye.

§

I was at the front entrance of the Club punctually at seven, as if I were as British as this building, which I read on its placard was established back in mid-nineteenth century, a grand old time to be British. I exchanged some dollars for rupees at an appallingly low rate, an unbreakable bad-habit of all hotels during all periods.

I was eager to have dinner with Krishna, not only for the promise of exquisite dinner offerings, but also to quiz him about myself and get some sort of clue about my past. My insouciance about my erstwhile identity was being replaced by curiosity, and I knew that, failing some sort of answers soon, it could become stressful and discomfiting, both of which annoyances I would have rather foregone.

Krishna's car and its very officious driver came for me within seconds of the appointed hour, proving definitively that Krishna was as much of a wannabe Brit as myself. Unlike the narrow compact "limousine" that picked me up at the airport, this was a vintage Rolls Royce with an articulated passenger section discreetly privatized from the driver by a tinted dividing window.

The soft luxury of the leather seats engulfed me as the car slid through the stately, crowded streets of the old Raj capital, which had so smoothly morphed into India's financial and entertainment hub after Liberation. Like all cities of its stature elsewhere, it has its share of steel and glass mega-structures, but never at the expense of destroying what made it great. The new buildings have been zoned so that they enhance what the Victorians left behind rather than dwarf them.

We drove along the breadth of the Queen's necklace, a corniche that flows between the sea and a sequenced row of luxurious housing, stretching from the cultural centre and five-star hotels of Nariman's Point to the south, up towards Malabar Hill on the northern edge of central Mumbai.

The Hill, once home to the spacious mini palaces of rich Gujarati and Pharsee Indians, has been transformed into condo-land with quality apartment high-rises for the immense Indian upwardly mobile middle classes, choking every available square inch of the area, eliminating its former leafiness, transforming it into a copy of New York's Upper East Side complete with exclusive clothing shops alongside Starbucks and pizza parlours. The only hold-out from the hubbub, Krishna's family heirloom mansion, built during some distant affluent century, sat on the edge of a lot large enough to build several condo-buildings, using the space instead as a tropical garden and a snaking driveway that culminated at the house.

The white-stone, two-story residence had obviously seen better days, but at least it was still standing. Krishna, dressed in a casual velvet smoking jacket with an emerald ascot as if he was posing for a Harrod's Christmas catalogue, was at the front portico to receive me. He took a drag from his cigarette in its meerschaum holder and broke out into a large smile.

"Welcome, while I'm still able to receive guests in my own house," he chuckled. "I am besieged to give it up. The conservationists want to turn it into a museum, while ten different speculators daily increase their offers to see which one will grab it and turn it into a gated community for the nouveau-riche. I must say, I am tempted. The latest offer was north of twenty-million sterling. But, I promised my grandfather...." He finally extended his hand for me to shake.

He led me into the rotunda-like reception area from which rose the obligatory alabaster staircase with its jet-black teak balustrade. He slowly walked me up the stairs, while filling me in on some family history. "We go back to Napoleonic times. Indian shipbuilders who first surfaced on the world stage by building the warships with which Nelson beat that Corsican upstart at Waterloo. But, we didn't reach our zenith until the eighteen-sixties and the end of the Opium Wars. It would seem that Britain humiliated and addicted an entire nation to opium, just so that my great-great-grandfather—you can see him here," he pointed to a humungous portrait of a bearded, costumed old man, "could become a billionaire by transporting the dreaded substance from Bombay to Shanghai. Yes, I must admit it, our family were high-scale dope dealers, but look at what it got us!"

We had reached the second floor and walked out onto an immense marble terrace with sculpted walls and parapets from which one could see the entirety of the festively lit Queen's Necklace and the reaches of the Indian Ocean, now speckled with the myriad lights of night-fishermen. "They're out there for pomfret," he explained before I could ask. "Bombay wouldn't be Bombay without its pomfret fish, and the tasty little buggers only bite after dark."

He showed me to a wicker chair that was contoured to the human behind by the many that had lounged in it to ruminate on their immense good fortune as they took in the view, drinking gin and tonics to soothe their malaria. He took the other chair and motioned with his hand. The drinks steward emerged from the shadows and placed a gourmet alcoholic's dream-tray on the marble table between us. There were two kinds of single malt whisky, a dusty jug of very old Port, an ice bucket, selected mixers, and most appropriately an azure-gleaming bottle of Bombay Sapphire gin. "I'll give you a little tour of the house by the by," he said, "but I thought alcohol on the terrace would be a good way to start our visit." The steward mixed a loaded Sapphire and tonic for me and poured a stiff shot of Glenlivet for his boss. "I love this terrace," he sighed. "It's one of the most compelling reasons to resist selling the house, even though it's draining me. I'm sure you can imagine what it costs to maintain a place this old. Notwithstanding the tidy chunk of capital I would have to trade with if I got rid of it outright. But, of course, the terrace, and... my grandfather to whom I swore on his deathbed I would never sell the house."

I hadn't said a word since I had arrived. It seemed imperative that I say something, but I knew that if I spoke it would only be to quiz him and discover what he knew about me. A difficult chore, which I had no idea how to broach. I retained a silence which

I tried to colour enigmatic with a half-raised smile. He waved his hand once more and a white-gloved snacks-wallah brought a silver tray of finger food. Crispy yet greaseless breaded-fried cauliflower and onion *pakoras* on an earthenware platter around a crystal-bowl of fiery dipping sauce, and a brass bowl of *chewda,* a salty-spicy mixture of roasted grains and pulses.

Krishna threw a small handful of *chewda* into his mouth and chased the frisky little snacks with a hearty sip of the whisky. Seeing that I wasn't about to say anything, he spread his palm towards me. "I don't know much about your family, but mine is one for the books. All that original money begat many generations of unabashed and rarely interrupted idleness, the only purpose of life to be tended hand and foot, and total license to be melancholy. No one in my family has had to do a shred of work in the last hundred years. I am an exception, and my father still cannot comprehend why I would want to get up in the morning and go to an office, even if it's inside the house. He has never done a single constructive thing in his life except to send me to schools and universities in England. He is incapable even of dressing himself without his valet. He has, since youth, spent most of his waking hours horizontal on a recliner listening to Mozart and meditating. The only reason he ever leaves the house is to visit the family trustee once a month, where he receives his benefits and immediately authorizes twice as much for expenses. Well, the money is drying out. We delivered our last batch of opium to China quite a while back. Frankly, if it weren't for the bits of money I bring in, the roof of this house would have long ago collapsed, most of the servants, including his valet, would have been sent home and the Rolls Royce would have shrunk into a Hyundai."

The breeze changed direction and brought with it a familiar perfume of flowers that only smell after dark as they sigh into the pitch-black sky of a tropical night. It brought back a memory. A large outdoor gathering. A garden lit up festively. A long buffet table. Everyone, men and women dressed in pinstripe suits and red ties. The same intoxicating scent.

"It was in Delhi, wasn't it? The lovely smell of the night-flowers. The tree must have been right over the buffet table where you and I talked about food. Isn't that right?"

"Jeff, please, I am a little familiar with the methods of traders such as yourself, even if the rest of your contacts are not. I am aware, for example, that you will reap information from the most trivial hints and involuntary admissions. But, let me go out on a limb here. Of course it was Delhi and its perfumed flowers and its terrible food that led to the two of us sitting on this terrace. I didn't that evening just promise you a good meal, I also promised you night-flowers. But that's all you'll get out of me. Not another word about Delhi, please." He downed his whisky as I bolted back the rest of my gin. I was thrilled. I did remember something and maybe I would remember more. "Another drink?" asked Krishna twittering his fingers in the direction of the tray.

"No," I said cheerfully. "Thanks, but I am famished. Maybe I can cash in on that meal you've been touting to me all up and down the Subcontinent."

"That's the spirit. Let's eat," announced my host, and sprung out of his chair to lead me back down the grand stairway into a regally dressed dining room with its impossibly tall ceilings.

"I hope I haven't been boring you with my family's inarguably undeserved wealth and its consequent indolence," apologized Krishna with self-deprecatingly raised eyebrows as he settled into the Louis Quinze chair.

"Everything that helps me to understand you better enriches my own vocabulary of experience," I assured him earnestly.

"Oh, my God. What have I done? You got me talking too much and will reap who-knows what benefits. But what's said is done, and now, let's not talk business any more, let's see what the chef proposes." He waved his hand yet a third different way, and two waiters appeared with the requisite accessories to justify this singular setting: silver trays, Bohemian china, white gloves, service from the left (removal from the right), all the essential little things that make the Krishnas of the world remain Krishna.

The meal began with Bombay Duck, not those dried-out fishy snacks one finds in India-towns, but the real thing, a mushy-bony fish, native to the Indian Ocean, that must be hand-picked of its bones, pressed for a few hours to firm up its flesh and then quick-fried. It ends up like an oval dumpling with crispy skin and a sweet-fleshed creamy interior that evaporates on contact with the tongue.

Next the main courses. A buttery eggplant puree, an innocently aromatic spinach and a rich yellow-lentil to accompany sweet-hot, coconut-milk and tomato based Mangalore fish-stew, redolent of garlic and curry leaf and chilies and a slew of compatible spices saucily around filets of pomfret, that ornery fish that only bites after dark. Alongside, for contrast, an incendiary, vinegary pork vindaloo from Catholic, ex-Portuguese Goa where pork is a birthright. To tame the curries, a mango, cucumber and fresh coriander yogurt *raita,* mounds of shiny saffron pilaf, and, I lost count, at least ten different freshly baked or fried breads, *puris, chapatis, kulchas* alongside an inventive array of stuffed *parathas.* For dessert, still warm *rajmalai,* the courtly *quenelles* of reduced-milk, pistachio and sweet-spice in a celebratory sauce speckled with real gold.

Krishna ate sparingly but drank many glasses of the exactingly chilled Chablis while explaining the intricacies of each dish in detail. There seemed no bounds to his desire to share what he knew, whether I responded or not, because in any case I had not much to add to the topic except vague memories of *tandoori* chicken and lamb *korma* in London restaurants as well as the watered down versions created for the uneducated palates that frequented the Yacht Club.

CHAPTER TWELVE

I asked to be dropped off on Apollo Bunder, the popular, seaside promenade near the Gate of India. This is a strip that sways like a palm tree, as lovers, walkers and thrill-seekers parade its length just for the heck of it, for a whiff of the incomparable and mysterious charm of their native city. I felt I would fit right in now that I had something to smile about, having correctly remembered that Delhi incident from my past, even if only sketchily.

I had just emerged from Krishna's priceless car, like a gentleman with the door held open for me by a liveried driver, when I came face to face with a dark-haired, middle-aged woman dressed in saris of various shades of black, a plumper, somewhat older version of the woman who had slapped me back in Istanbul. I winced at the memory but it must have looked like a smile because she approached me venomously, and spat on the ground. "What are you smiling at, you son of a bitch! After what you did to my sister!" she cried in Hindi. Upon which she slapped me hard and hurried off to meld into the crowd, much as the first woman had done.

Unlike my reaction in Istanbul, this time the slapping got me angry. I turned to find some support from the driver, but he had already rushed back to his wheel and was niftily pulling into traffic. Great! Not only was I mad as hell, but I had no one to complain to. Seething, I walked to the parapet and started screaming at the night sea that swelled and subsided like a huge puddle of oil. I let go full-vent, angry at the unfairness of it all. At its one-sidedness. How could just about everyone around me in two different countries on two different continents know so much about me, when all I could recall were some minor, trivial details about a boring business event in Delhi. My earlier contentment became vapour, exacerbating my fury.

I must have screamed for several minutes, because it started to hurt my throat. I felt a small hand on my shoulder. I turned ready to strike and then I gasped. Miryam, the same elven girl from Istiklal Caddesi who had saved me from the original slapping incident, was right there for the sequel, freshly like a vision in a silver full-length sheath with enticing slits on the sides and a crown of scarlet feathers on long platinum tresses.

"What's up, cowboy? Bad guy stole your stake?"

I broke out in a loud laugh. "You, again!" I exclaimed, instead of something more suitable like, "I am so very happy to see you," or "You're the only bright light in my morbid life," or even better, "I love you, I don't know how you keep finding me, will you marry me?"

She winked at me. I could have sworn she levitated for a twinkling instant, performed a quick grand *jeté* and landed on the point. "So, is now a good time to go dancing?"

"Lead the way," I implored as I tried to hug her.

She flitted away from my embrace. "Not yet, big guy. Come on, the music is playing and the night is young."

§

I woke up in a panic. The cavernous Yacht Club room had swallowed my little Miryam. I was alone in a bed that had granted me sexual pleasure unimaginable by mere mortals, and surely more intense than I had ever had whether I could prove it or not.

It was a limitless thirst for her affection that had been tunefully sparked in an ersatz disco down a side street from Apollo Bunder. "It's no big deal as a dance club, but at least we have it," she had apologized as we hit the floor. We danced for what seemed an eternity, never resting. Abba's *Dancing Queen,* Gloria Gaynor's *I Will Survive,* Lipps' *Funkytown*; anthemic disco, yesterday's beat, at obscene volume, taking turns to rouse us, to keep us gyrating, segueing into other iconic songs. We danced tirelessly, stopping only briefly to shoot down mouthfuls of liquor at the bar, until we collapsed simultaneously to the floor in breathless giggles. How we got back to the Yacht Club, climbed the marble stairs, threw off our clothes and jumped into bed was rather hazy in my head, but I was remembering every lusty moment of our shared desire, the pure silk of her slender body, the sweet taste of her mouth, the firmness of her breasts, the rigid pinkness of her nipples, the euphoria of being inside her, scared that I would injure her yet locked in place with urgency by her interlocked arms, her palpable rapture... it had lasted a long time, I had kept at it, elated by her repeated climaxes, her beseeching eyes for more, until I was aching and finally had my own climax in torrential jets. It was as if we had finally made love after waiting just about forever since we had first wanted to do it. We must have rolled off each other and fallen asleep after that, because next thing I remember was waking up by myself with a yearning to at least kiss her good morning, but she was no longer there, only her leftover scent of jasmine and musk.

A knock on the door excited me, hoping it was her returning, but it was the morning steward with my breakfast. A tarnished silver-plated tray loaded with facsimiles of all the British favourites: greasy eggs and bacon, cold toast, tasteless marmalade, weak coffee, even watered down oatmeal, and an Indian broadsheet on the side.

I nibbled distractedly as I perused the newspaper for my first glimpse of the world outside the confines of my own mind. It was dated January 9, 2009. It shocked me that I hadn't so far bothered to know the date since it is such a signifier of being part of society and it must have been as important to me as it is to everyone else.

The top half of the front page was devoted to the ongoing story of the Mumbai terrorist attack of December and the active hunt for its perpetrators. Half of the lower half was plastered with accounts of the worldwide economic meltdown and its refusal to recuperate in any kind of hurry. The other lower half was devoted to the new president of the United States whose inauguration was a mere eleven days away and whose political agenda promised not only a cure-all for the ills of the planet but also greater access to the American Dream, by definition an impossible combination of goals. I flipped the page and my attention was drawn to a colour photo of someone who remotely resembled me. It was a story about a rogue trader named Stephen Hunter who had bankrupted a long-established bank, trading out of Singapore with speculative transactions that were deemed criminal. Various countries had issued warrants for his arrest. I wondered if it could possibly be me and examined the photograph more closely. To my relief, I noticed that Hunter had brown eyes and thinning hair. Decidedly unlike me.

CHAPTER THIRTEEN

Breakfast barely over, there was another knock at my door. This time certain it was Miryam returning, I rushed to open it. Facing me were two armed policemen in crumpled beige uniforms and regulation headgear, burly and sweating, standing slightly apart to allow a sightline to the woman who had slapped me last night, a step behind them. She was agitated; they impassive. They apologized for the intrusion in accents that imitated Peter Sellers' imitation Indian accent in *The Party,* and politely asked me to accompany them to the station to clear up "a matter."

"What matter?" I tried to sound impatient but observant of their authority.

"It's only a small matter, sir, a trivial matter indeed," they said with even more authority, as the Slapper observed me like she would a snake in a pit.

"I'm rather busy. Can we not settle this trivial matter some other time?" I hedged.

"No, we cannot," screeched the Slapper from the background. "Now! Now that we have you!"

The policemen blinked in helplessness and motioned to me to shut up and come along. I was not looking forward to whatever was in store, but I was glad that it would at least offer further clues to my past life. We walked the long block to the station in silence, four abreast, with me and the Slapper on either end to keep us away from each other.

The station was bedlam with a small squadron of transvestite hustlers in full sari and fake eyelashes, freshly arrested and being noisily processed. My heart sank thinking we would have to wait through all that, but being a high-ranking suspect, a Master Yachtsman, I was led to the air-conditioned office of the chief and offered tea while awaiting his pleasure.

He entered a fashionable fifteen minutes later, smartly dressed in an ironed uniform, many jeweled rings, pomaded grey hair, kohl-outlined melancholy eyes, and a strong smell that surprisingly I was able to identify as attar-of-rose, a specialty of Lucknow. He sat at the edge of his seat, and looked at us wearily. He motioned his men to the back of the room. Now free to approach, the Slapper made a move towards me. I braced myself for another slap, which I knew I would have to bear without being able to reciprocate.

The Chief ordered her to sit down. "So, what's this all about, cousin Rachna? Why have you brought me this gentleman?"

Rachna spoke the details of her complaint in rapid-fire Hindi. "This man is no gentleman. He is a cad and a bandit. A *dacoit*! He persuaded my sister Varsha to marry him, embezzled her entire fortune to use for his gambling, fathered four children, and one day, with NO warning, he abandoned all of them to the mercy of the winds, to the charity of the family, to beds on the streets, to begging for their food, the incorrigible SCOUNDREL, the damnable DEVIL, the–"

"–None of that is true!" I chimed in Hindi. "I had never in my life seen this woman or her sister, until each of them attacked me in two different countries and slapped me on the face unprovoked."

"Oh, we had plenty of provocation, cousin Ashok," said Rachna, addressing the chief. "And here's the proof!" She dug into her handbag and produced a stack of photographs, which she adroitly flicked so that they spread across the desk in an attractive pattern. They were snapshots, all of them with me in them, arm in arm with the Istanbul version of Rachna, hugging and playing with four, young, very dark-haired children.

Ashok looked closely at a photograph with all four of the children. "But, cousin Rachna, these look like Indian children," he complained.

"Of course they look Indian. Their mother is Indian. But look at their eyes: blue-gray all of them, just like their father, this… this *Mister* Jefferson Cooper!"

"Yes, I see," nodded Ashok. "Well it's clear-cut and well proven then, cousin Rachna. Thank you for bringing this criminal to our attention, and now please let us deal with him in our own official way. You can go with a clear conscience. You have performed your duty."

"Yes, fine, I will go. As long as you don't forget to invite me to the execution!" She stood up. "I'll take back the photographs."

"No, no. They are state evidence, now." Ashok stood up to bring his open palms together in front of his chest in *namaste* to her and expedite her departure. She *namaste'ed* back at him, threw one final poisonous glance at me, and took her leave.

Ashok motioned for his men to go outside and shut the door. He turned to me with an understanding smile. "More tea, or would you prefer a shot of Scotch?" he said in English, in some sort of Midland accent.

He took me by surprise. "Tea'll be f-fine," I stammered.

He got up to pour my tea while he talked to me over his shoulder. "It's no crime, Mister Cooper, to abandon a wife and children. Many of us would gladly do it if we had the nerve. It is also no crime to spend a wife's money. In fact, it's almost our duty to do so." He brought me the tea and peered at me. "That is, if you indeed were married to my cousin, or, as you'd have us believe, you were not. The photos, well, we all know about Photoshop, don't we? Your image looks like it doesn't even belong in too many of these pictures." He sat down and picked up a couple of the photographs to show me.

"The colour of the children's eyes… again, it can be Photoshop, or it can be a coincidence. We do have people with blue-grey eyes in this country. In Ladakh. Possibly those children had a Ladakhi father. Come to think of it, cousin Rachna's husband is Ladakhi." He shook his head. "Please, finish your tea, and you can be on your way. I have been given no grounds to hold you. On the other hand, you must have misbehaved in some terrible way against my cousins for them to want to punish you so intercontinentally and so imaginatively. Whatever it is, when I find out you'll be hearing from me. Good-bye, Mister Cooper." He *namaste'ed* without even looking at me. His men entered as if silently summoned and I scampered to my feet.

"Thank you," I muttered, as I quickly turned and returned to freedom.

§

I retreated to my room and double-locked the door. I hadn't checked my money since I had been here. It was all accounted for, both the carry-on and the secret compartment of the suitcase being still suitably full of cash. I lay back on my bed. It had been a long night of love-making and I had got up way too early and had far too much excitement. I shut my eyes and instantly fell asleep fully dressed.

I woke up at dusk. The sky from my balcony was a sultry mauve and the hefty silhouette of the Gate dark and powerful against it. Despite all else inexplicable that should have been my concern, all I could focus on was my insatiable desire for Miryam. I dressed quickly, with a pert matching of white linen pants, pink silk shirt and green socks with sandals.

I parked myself on the exact spot of Apollo Bundra where she had found me the previous night. I waited for close to two hours, smoking a whole pack of cigarettes as night settled in and the seaside promenade filled up with its usual kibitzers. Finally desperate, I walked down the side street that I thought was the one with the dancing club. I was wrong. I circled back up to the promenade and tried another street. On my third try I found it. It was completely empty except for the bored barman, who instantly snapped to his welcoming stance when I entered.

"I am so happy to see you are still here," he beamed, remembering my hefty tips from our last encounter. "Way you are dancing with that Miryam lady last night, sure, I thought, he goes with her."

"Goes?" My heart fluttered. "Goes, where?" I asked, probably a bit too loudly, too broken-heartedly.

"Varkala, my good friend. In Kerala. Small place. You find easy. She has great house, very good view, she has shown me in photographs."

I tossed him a hundred dollar tip and rushed back to my room. I grabbed my bags and checked out of the Yacht Club, telling reception I had been summoned to Delhi and must fly there tonight. I lied to them because I didn't want anyone to know where I was really going. For once I wanted to be as anonymous as I felt. I stopped the Yacht Club taxi after only a few blocks. I paid him the full fare to the airport and waited for him to drive out of sight. I flagged another taxi and headed to the central bus station. In India, the best way to get lost and untraceable is to travel by bus.

CHAPTER FOURTEEN

It would have taken only two hours to reach Varkala by plane if I had wanted to use my passport and advertise my whereabouts. Instead, by bus, it took more like thirty-six hours via Bangalore and Trivandrum. It tired me to the core; I felt drunk. I chose the least scruffy rickshaw driver with a sincere smile and asked him to take me to a quiet hotel.

"Beachside? Cliffside?" He asked, as if I should know. Then I remembered that the barman said she had a view.

"Which has more view?" I asked in Malayalam to make sure he understood me.

"Cliffside, of course," his smile widening.

"Let's go then."

By luck he turned out a good person and took me to a decent place with a clean room inside a papaya grove, a steel strongbox for my money, a firm bed with soft sheets. And they understood totally that I didn't want to show them a passport, as long as I pre-paid in cash.

§

According to the brochure at the hotel lobby, the cliffside of Varkala is a playful meander some five hundred feet above a powerful sweep of Indian Ocean, whose golden sands and graceful white-caps make for a painterly backdrop to the gentle resort up-top. The formerly sleepy village developed quickly into an alternate-life-stylers' haven, as Kovalam, the original Kerala beach hotspot, became over-crowded and disheveled. Varkala stepped into the breach with a string of relaxed restaurants, jewelry stores, *ayurvedic* massage clinics, dentists, and yoga retreats set along a paved path hugging the cliff's edge, with the ever-present ocean-scape below.

I sat at an empty table right up front, occasionally stroking my wallet and my passport, making sure they were still with me, and had a cup of spicy-milky *chai,* staring at the view same as everyone else. Unlike the rest of them, my mind was not at ease. I was in desperate need of finding my Miryam and no notion of how to go about it. I considered a proper search, either by poking around and describing her, which would raise interest and sabotage the anonymity I had so painstakingly maintained; or I could walk endlessly up and down the path and along the numberless little alleys leading to the interior of the village in a haphazard and probably futile quest. I decided to stay put right at that table, drinking tea after tea, smoking many packs of cigarettes, and let her find me. She had been successful twice already, so why not a third time....

On the third straight day of my vigil I began to lose heart. All manner of doubt darkened my horizon. Possibly that barman had lied to me or was misinformed. Or then again, she was such a mercurial imp she might have already left for another spot. Worse yet, that I was not meant to find her, that I was doomed to miss out on my shot at a happiness with which to sweeten my insufferable loneliness, my debilitating confusion.

I called the waiter to pay for my tea, and looked up and down the path one more time. There she was, some thirty yards up towards the sunset point of the cliff. She was peering right at me, with a twinkle of apology in her eyes for making me wait to make sure I truly loved her. Her long blond hair undulating in the breeze, her gossamer, blindingly white dress clinging to her perfect body, she winked and turned into an alley, slowly so that I could catch up. I followed her carefully from some distance so that no one could guess the connection between us. She stopped at the garden entrance of a little cottage and undid the padlock, which she left dangling. She quickly crossed the garden and entered the cottage.

I reached the gate and looked furtively up and down the alley. It was deserted. I slipped in and locked the padlock behind me.

I snuck into the cottage as imperceptibly as I could. I shut and latched the door. My eyes adjusted from the harsh sunshine to the soft light inside. The wide room was simple, almost bare, with all-white adobe and colourful Rajasthani pillows and fabrics, a low table, a soft bed covered in silk, and wide patio doors on the back wall opening to the sunset over the ocean. The air smelled of jasmine and musk: she was near. She appeared from behind a curtain, laughing musically. She was a vision in her golden nakedness. I took her in my arms gingerly. We kissed the openmouthed kiss of lovers starved for each other.

§

The first breakfast, as would every other breakfast of a delirious month with Miryam, was set up for me on a little secluded terrace behind the house, perched on the very edge of the cliff, high above the ever mutating patterns of the surf. English china, embroidered tablecloth somewhat faded from repeated hand-washing, fluffy *paratha,* a different one every day–onion, potato, saffron, plain, depending on Miryam's mood–coffee direct from Bangalore, the only place in India where they understand the life-affirming bean, tropical fruit at its peak ripeness sliced and dusted with chilies, and at the end of the repast, meaningful glances, tender hand caresses and a mutually passionate trip to bed, she holding onto my shoulders, I lifting her to my chest by the buttocks, for hungry sex, as if neither of us had ever before been in love.

After the sex of that first breakfast, Miryam excused herself to run an errand, suggesting I stay put and wait for her, as if I had any intention of going anywhere. I spent an hour showering and then sitting in the sun to dry off, fretting about her and wondering how and when to go fetch my suitcase and my money from the hotel and get it done undetected. I shouldn't have wasted my time thinking about it. Miryam returned with a porter who carried my suitcase on his head, while she carted my carry-bag on her shoulder. She dismissed the porter with a tip at the little gate and struggled with the suitcase to the cottage door which I had opened for her.

"There, now you can change your clothes," she complained as she dropped the suitcase on the floor. "And really, Cooper, you shouldn't be carrying such obscene sums of money, someone might get ideas," she teased as she tossed the carry-on to my arms.

I opened the clasp to find it stuffed with the same old bundles of hundred dollar bills. "How did you get the strongbox open?" I asked, not entirely sure I wanted to find out.

"Oh, we have our ways," she snickered and disappeared into the bathroom. I heard the shower splashing on her perfect body. I envied its intimacy with her. I wanted to be that shower.

§

She rolled a large spliff, piles of hash held together with only thin strands of tobacco. She lit it and took a deep toke. She passed it to me as she exhaled a blue-grey plume that lingered in the air spicily.

"I don't think I should," I said as I held the joint. "I am confused enough as is."

"Exactly. Things can only get better, am I right?"

I inhaled the intoxicating smoke and held it inside like someone somewhere must have shown me in the past. "I'm not just confused, you know," I started to confess as I exhaled an equally long plume. "I am so lost it frightens me. I am someone because of you in this house, but if you were to disappear on me for some reason, I'd be no one again. I don't know how long I can go on like this."

"Then it must be time to do something, isn't it?"

"Do?"

"Help you."

§

"Let's start at the beginning," she suggested with a glint through eyeglasses I had not seen her wear before.

"My life began that awful evening in Istanbul when you rescued me from total desperation," I responded matter-of-factly.

"That's very nice of you to say, but it really started a couple of days earlier, didn't it?"

"If you can call it a start," I complained. "I woke up entirely disoriented and anonymous in some village outside Bodrum, and I just kept going until you saw me."

"The key, then, would have to be why you were in that Bodrum village in the first place."

"It was probably to find you," I smiled.

"No, it wasn't," she declared definitively. "Judging from your huge amount of cash, I'd say you went there to hide."

"From whom?" I wondered aloud.

"From whomever you stole the money," she shrugged.

"It's as simple as that?"

"Usually is," she shrugged again. "Money does that."

"Maybe it was from that woman who slapped me in Istanbul, and whose sister accused me in Bombay."

"Aah, a woman...." she smiled knowingly.

"Well, I have no memory of it."

"Or, you don't want to remember."

"That occurred to me," I conceded.

"And?"

"I don't see how anyone can willfully forget the facts of one's life."

"And yet you remember everything else. Languages, food, geography, money, love, smells... especially smells." She took a deep breath. I wondered if she was smelling me. "Let's go back much further. Let's go back to the very beginning."

"You're sounding like a shrink. Are you a shrink?"

"I am many things, my darling Cooper. Right now, however, all I am is your devoted lover who is determined to make you happy."

"That in itself makes me happy."

"Thank you," she said somewhat impatiently. "So, think. All the way back to the cradle. Even to the womb."

"It was dark in there."

"And then there was light. Wasn't there?"

"I suppose there must have been."

"And you were cuddled in your mother's arms, sucking on her breast. What did she smell like?"

"I have no memory of such a thing."

"Sure you do. Everyone does."

"Maybe my life didn't start that way. Maybe my mother died giving birth, or had to give me up for adoption."

"If either of those possibilities were true it would explain a lot. Come on. Try harder. You're coming out of the darkness and you're in some kind of little bed. Is someone picking you up? Is someone hugging you to protect you from the world?"

"No. Definitely no such memory."

"Did you have to lie in that crib a long time?"

"Now that you mention it, yes!"

"What makes you think so?"

"I don't know. But I do remember sleeping in a crib for endless hours. Yes, I do. And I remember thinking that it was boring."

"You're kidding with me, but I believe we're getting somewhere."

"Do I get a lollipop?"

"No. You get a kiss."

§

"The smells I remember most vividly are all unpleasant. Shit and piss and something to do with hospitals."

"Let's flash forward. Say, to your second birthday."

"There was no second birthday. That is certain."

"How so?"

"I am very partial to the numeral 'two.' I would remember anything to do with two."

"Even though you say you remember nothing at all?"

"But that can't possibly be true, right?"

"What is it about the numeral 'two'?"

"Things come in pairs. You and I, for example. I have two feet, two hands, two eyes, two ears. I have lived two lives. The one before and the one now. And more, much more...."

"Okay, fine. How about your third birthday?"

I thought hard. I wanted to please her. I wanted to give her something for all her effort. "There was a cake on my third birthday. It smelled remotely of strawberries–"

"–Because they were out of season. Because your birthday is in January–"

"–I think that my real birthday is in June. They were strawberries on the cake, but they wouldn't give me any of it, it wasn't for me, it was for the kid at the next table. That is why I said 'remote.'"

"Are you really remembering that, or are you teasing me?" She caressed my face.

"I remember *that*! Someone caressing my face."

"A woman? Your mother?"

"No, a man. An older man. Who smelled of tobacco and whisky. He caressed my face."

"Did you like that?"

"At first I did, but he went on touching me everywhere. I remember it hurt. No, I didn't like that. Not at all."

"What did you do?"

"I couldn't do much, could I? I was three."

§

"Let's play a game," she said with a glint in her eyes. We had just woken up after a post-coital afternoon nap. The sun was getting ready to set. The sky was a mess of reds and purples. The ocean below us swelled in a long wave that broke mid-surf and rolled onto the beach like frothy meringue. She was behind me, gently tickling my back first with her fingertips, then her nipples, in rhythm with the wave. "Let's pretend we are eight years old–"

"–and they catch us nude in bed," I giggled as I succumbed to the pleasures of her touch.

"No, no no. We are outside. And it is sunny."

"No. Not sunny much. Mostly cloudy. And rain. Much rain. Stormy. I remember being wet a lot. Of that I'm certain."

"We are indoors then."

"Definitely."

"And what are we doing?"

"*We?*"

"Yes. We. You and me. Play with me. It'll help you. Say anything that comes to your head."

"Yes. Let's do play. How about draw poker? We always played poker, you and me."

"And who's winning?"

"I am. I taught you the game. I win just about every hand. Except when I let you, to keep you interested."

"Let me?"

"Like when you pull lucky. That time you got a straight flush after you drew two cards. Who gets a straight flush drawing two cards, for Christ's sake?!"

"What did you have?"

"Dead-man's pairs. Aces over eights. A better than average hand."

"You have no trouble remembering all that?"

"Not at all. Clear as a bell."

§

We smoked a big joint with our afternoon tea. For snacks she served thin *dosa* pancakes with spicy dipping *sambar* on the side. We had drawn the curtain. After fifteen consecutive days the view had become trite, like a film you've seen too many times.

"How old should we be today," I asked in-between tender, perky mouthfuls.

"Let's say... twelve," she said randomly. "We're still playing poker and it's still raining. Are we nude yet?"

"Almost."

"So where do you think we are? All that rain."

"I've been trying to figure that out. It's the States, fairly sure. You'd think it would be the northwest, or the northeast. One or the other. Maybe Vermont, maybe Oregon. All that rain. But it is neither. Because it might be stormy but it's also stifling hot. It is the southwest. Or maybe Texas. Yes. Texas. Do you have any ideas?"

"Me? No." She laughed. "I wasn't even born yet when you were twelve. I have no idea. I wasn't there at all, you know that, don't you? This is only a game."

"Oh, you were there, alright. You've always been there for me. Otherwise I would have refused to live."

"Why are we *almost* nude?"

"Well, we're playing strip-poker up in the tree-house, you see. Trouble is, I'm winning as usual, so you're, like, stark naked, and I'm trying my best to lose so that I too can be naked, but no way. I bet my shirt on king-high and you lose with queen-high. It was a struggle."

"And why are you trying so hard to lose your shirt?"

"Oh, you know...."

§

Slowly, far too slowly for Miryam's liking, tiny, barely connected memories were being induced to appear in my mind. Nothing earth-shattering, and nowhere close to the core events of my identity, but encouraging none the less. At least to me. Miryam, who had obviously made it some kind of mission to revive the entirety of the unexpurgated lexicon of my existence was less pleased. Her newest method to coax remembrances out of me was to deny me sexually. Whereas our lovemaking had previously been a boundless sharing of unrestricted favours, it had now been reduced to expedited orgasms and a cheerless "good night." When I complained, she made it clear: "You start trying a little harder and so will I."

"Performance-based bonus," I blurted.

"Does that tell you anything?"

"Something. Not sure what."

"Think," she said and took my hand to lead me to bed and reward me for what she considered a breakthrough event. I didn't quite see the significance of what I had said, but I was happy she did.

§

We got out of bed reluctantly, as I kissed her again and again milking the resurgence of our unrestricted passion to the hilt, lest it might fizzle out were my "performance" to falter anew.

"Come, come," she coaxed me as she ran her fingers through my hair that had grown longer during the month and now crowned my face in brown-blondish wavelets. "A good friend is coming to see us. He is a trained yogi, a holy man and an authority on renewing ruined lives. He's from Kovalam but now lives in Santa Barbara, where just about everyone needs his help. Michael Jackson, for example. And just about every investment banker worth the title. His name used to be Balan, but now he's known as Bill."

We barely had time to shower and dress when there was a gentle knock on the door. She greeted Bill with a modest bow and a *namaste*. He looked the least like any Indian holy man I could picture. Brand new Nikes, immaculate track suit, stylish haircut and the latest in fashion sunglasses drooping on the bridge of his nose so that he could look at you straight if he felt like it, or down through the dark lenses if he didn't. He looked at me through the lenses. I put out my hand in a Western-style handshake.

"Aah, dude, no *namaste*," he smiled in a California accent. "You must be 'Merican.'"

"I'm not sure," I said with sincerity after briefly sharing limp-fish contact with his soft hand.

"Well, okay, let's dig in and find out, shall we?"

Somehow I knew that I really shouldn't let this brash, newfangled yogi dig into my affairs at all. Somehow my gut feeling was to dislike him outright. But Miryam seemed to trust him unreservedly. She fussed, making him comfortable, and then repaired to the kitchen to prepare tea and leave us to get acquainted.

"So, Cooper," he said, finally looking me in the eyes having removed the sunglasses.

"So-o, Bill," I responded, and waited for him to speak again.

"I would like to tell you two stories, and you can listen or not as you like, and you can draw conclusions or not as you like, and then tell me what you think or not as you like. Okay?"

"I want to listen, certainly I'll listen. And if I'm smart enough to draw any conclusions, I'll certainly share them with you. I'm troubled, as you probably know, and I'm grateful for any help I can get."

"Alrighty. Here goes: The first story is about a rich man, a banker, a ruthless man his entire life, a real fuck-face, a creep, wouldn't even help his own children, all but one of whom died from being too poor to seek proper medical attention when they got ill. Naturally, his one survivin' child wanted *nada* to do with him, refusin' all contact, it's like he doesn't exist. So now, old and all alone, he finds out he has cancer and will very soon be checkin' out. He decides to try and finally become a good person. He is sick and all, but he can still get around sort-of, and he goes to the slums of Bombay, a city where he has lived all his life and never once saw the misery that exists in the heart of it. He is appalled. He's, like, really really grossed-out. Every sort of human depravity everywhere he turns, like nonstop slaps on the face. 'Alright,' he thinks. 'Here's a place my money can do some good.' He returns the next day with a couple of assistants carrying billions of rupees in cash, almost all his money minus a few thousand to pay his doctors in his final days. And he starts dishin' it out by the bushel. People line up, there are incidents as they beat up on each other tryin' to get at the money before it runs out, a couple of 'em get trampled almost to death, it's a mess, but somehow it works out. He manages to hand out all the money, and everyone in the slum gets a bit of it, and then with the last of his strength he gets himself back to the hospital. But as luck would have it, instead of dyin', he improves! He gets better and better, and with a bit more of the excellent doctorin' he was affordin' up to that point, he would probably have totally recovered. Except that the money he had kept behind dries up, and they throw him out of the private hospital and he has to go to a public hospital. Now, I don't know if you're aware, but a public hospital in this country is someplace you don't want to end up if you're seriously ill. And just as had happened to his kids back when they were sick and he wouldn't give 'em any money, he gets the same kind of mistreatment and gets sick again, not enough to kill him right off but not exactly in any kind of enviable position either, if you know what I mean. Nevertheless he is well enough to be discharged from the public hospital, they need the bed for someone else to be admitted and die in unhappy agony, and he ends up not only sick but also homeless. Broke and weak, he returns to the slum, hopin' the people he had given so much money to would take care of him, or at least give him a bed to sleep on. Naturally, those people are still very poor, despite the free lunches they had got from 'im, and have no gratitude in their hearts, not a speck. No one will even look at 'im. He ends up on the streets, a beggar among the thousands of other beggars, and he lives on for about a year in abject poverty and turmoil, until he throws himself into the sea and drowns, yet another anonymous victim of India's inability to take care of its own." Bill shut his eyes and extended his hand towards me to invite my reactions.

"Obviously," I started to say, then reconsidered. "No, not obviously. There is nothing obvious here. It's a rare story about a very rare person. And it's not really believable either. I can't see anyone being that mean to begin with, and having been smart enough to become so very rich, turn entirely stupid at the end and give away just about all his money to the poor. The only obvious thing in this situation is that you cannot help anyone by giving them a little chunk of free money. They just squander it and are just as poor right away after it's gone."

"You are so right, Cooper. You see, you understand life very well, even if you claim you're unable to remember any of the probably unpleasant details of your own life. But you're wrong about the old man not bein' believable. He's very very real, of that I'm abso-fuckin-lutely sure, because he was my own father and I his one survivin' child."

"I... I am sorry to hear that," I whispered, because he had managed to surprise me and I could think of nothing else to say.

"And I'm happy to hear you say that. It's the first honest and spontaneous reaction you've had so far. And I'm sorry to disappoint you, but in fact you were right in the first place. The story was made up and totally outrageous. No one could be that mean or that stupid as the old man I described, just like you said."

"Now, you're confusing me," I blurted.

At that moment Miryam came to my rescue with the tea service. "Good," he said offhandedly as he sipped some of his tea. "Now we're gettin' somewhere. And here's my second and final story. I gotta tell you in advance that this one is in fact, no kiddin', a *true* story, and I want you to pay close attention. Anyway, it's brief."

I smiled and decided to give him his due. Maybe he wasn't such a quack as I had made him out to be. I nodded and extended my own hand to encourage him to continue.

"Again I shall talk of an Indian person, but this time it's a woman and her story takes place in Istanbul, far away from home. She is of 'a certain age,' slightly past her prime but still very sexy and lively, with a nice little bundle that she inherited from her father, livin' high off the hog in Beyoglu, within easy reach of all kinds of good-looking young guys who are permanently on the prowl down on Istiklal Caddesi. She is havin' a great little time using the guys one at a time, not that they mind bein' used since she treats 'em well, but discards them when they get too cheeky, goin' on to the next dude and the next, there is such an endless supply. And then, the worst happens to her. She meets someone, a foreigner, and she commits the fatal error of 'fallin' in love.' He's about ten years younger, very handsome, a bit like you, and he's accommodatin' too because she's very affectionate with him, she adores him and he enjoys that. He has come to Istanbul, from where he never tells her, and leaves just as suddenly, and this is good for her since their time together is so very intense that she needs the break to recover and to yearn for his next return, anticipation itself being a sheer pleasure because she's fearin' that every time he leaves, he'll never return. But he *does* come back and she is so blinded with her love, or lust, call it what you will, that she totally surrenders, falling prey to his continuous, but obviously disingenuous declarations of endless love. And then, a truly terrible thing happens. On the third, and *last* of his visits he is depressed and unhappy and tells her of some kind of money problem he's havin', and persuades her to 'lend' him money, all that she has, promising her a good return, many times the amount, in less than no time. She trusts him, she's lovelorn right? And like an idiot she hands over her security blanket and he leaves with her money, never to return, never to repay a penny." Bill took off his sunglasses and looked at me sternly, accusingly.

"I guess, I know this woman. She was the one that slapped me in Istanbul, wasn't she?" I turned to Miryam.

"Do you remember her?" asked Miryam casually.

"Yes, yes, I do," I admitted. It felt as if I had just been stabbed in the head by some kind of ice-pick. "I remember her very well. I remember being with her. And… and I must have taken her money, if you say so. I think I remember something about money, I'm not sure. But why? And how? I have no clue. Did I just steal it?"

"No, you didn't," said Bill, replacing the sunglasses on the bridge of his nose. "You're not a thief. Not really."

"So what did I do? If not really a thief, then what? Tell me, please!"

"It's not for me to say. You're the one that should be telling us."

"I can't! I really don't know. And if I know, I don't remember!" I felt cornered. I felt nauseous.

"I'm done here," said Bill drily, as he stood up. He *namaste'ed* to both of us and made a quick exit.

I darted upright. I looked at Miryam in total despair. "I really don't know what to do! What should I do?"

She stood on tip-toe and brushed my lips with a feathery kiss. "Don't sweat it," she smiled encouragingly. "It'll come to you."

CHAPTER FIFTEEN

I slept fitfully, waking every hour or so to make sure that Miryam's arms were still around me. It was as if I knew something dreadful was afoot, that my month-long romantic fantasy was at an end. In the morning I found myself alone in bed, which was not unusual, since Miryam made a habit of letting me sleep in while she made breakfast. What was unusual was that there weren't the normal morning smells in the air. No aroma of coffee, no wafts of *paratha* from the frying pan. No musk. No jasmine.

I wrapped a *lungi* around me and rushed out to the balcony. The view of the ocean was the only thing that was as it had always been. The breakfast table was bare, no English bone china, no food, not even a tablecloth. Just a couple of cups of what looked suspiciously like Nescafe and an overweight woman wrapped in colourful lightweight scarves smoking a flavourful French cigarette, sitting with her back to me. No Miryam!

"Good morning, Mr Cooper," said the woman without turning around.

I approached the table tentatively. "Aishe?" I asked in shock, her identity confirmed by a familiar scent of piss and stale perfume that was now reaching my nose.

She turned her head an inch to beckon me to the seat beside her. "Of course it's me. Aren't I always there for you when you need an airplane ticket?"

I darted to the front to face her head-on. "Where's Miryam? What have you done to her?!"

"Me? My dear man, I don't *do* anything to people, except get them where they need to get to. Miryam is gone. Such a funny creature, you never know where she'll flit to next." She had switched to French, I guess to soften the blow and make it sound a bit more mellifluous.

"And what the hell are you doing here?" I asked as I took the seat opposite her. Deflated. Defeated. I took a sip of the instant coffee. It added to my depression. I spat it out.

"Terrible coffee, but what can we do? Miryam took her good coffee with her. It's one of her quirks. Can't go anywhere without it. Anyway, it doesn't much matter. You're leaving today also."

"Oh?"

"Yes. The vacation is over, my dear Jeff."

"And who the hell are you to tell me?" I was feeling cornered with serious premonitions of trouble.

"I'm the travel agent and the messenger. Please don't shoot me. I have no blame. And please stop using the 'H' word, I hate it. I'm sure I'll get there soon enough, there is no reason to remind me." She was back to English, the best language on earth for frank talk and exchange of bad news.

"Alright, I'm curious. What's all this about?"

"Oh, about two billion dollars, and more specifically approximately a hundred and fifteen thousand in cash. And Interpol. And Scotland Yard. And a few other police departments around the planet. And warrants for your arrest in an array of languages. And an overdue appearance of yours to explain why you'd flee all over the place instead of facing your accusers like a man and taking your medicine regardless of how bitter it might taste. You did after all cause your own… disease, if I may call it that."

"I have no idea what you're talking about," I said, even though some of the ugly truth was beginning to surface through the clouds of my forgetfulness.

"You might have been able to hide for a whole lot longer, you know. Maybe even forever. Were it not for Hussein, your funny little employee. One must really be very very careful who one hires as confidant. Very very careful."

"Hussein?" I echoed. Then I remembered the odd fellow from that restaurant back in Istanbul, and his intriguing note, his sudden departure. "What about him?" I asked, though I had already guessed the answer.

"Well, he's a snoopy, sneaky pest, isn't he? He had uncovered all your secrets when you weren't looking. He knew your true identity. And when the police nailed him he tried to save his own skinny behind by spilling everything to them. Though, you'll be happy to know, he is securely in a Turkish jail now for many more years than await you. The Turks take a lot less kindly to conspirators than the English will with you."

"I think it's time you told me what you know," I said resignedly and prepared myself for the worst by taking a big gulp of the Nescafe and even swallowing it, like those sacrificial victims of the Aztecs used to do with unsweetened chocolate in preparation for the inevitable: anything being better that another sip of the bitter potion.

It didn't take long for Aishe to relate her facts about myself, and, as my past started piecing itself together in her narrative, I realized that I really must have been trying to submerge the shame and hopelessness of it in a state of willful amnesia. I didn't immediately recall quite everything she said, but enough of it came back to trust that she was telling the truth.

At the end of it she presented me with a ticket to London from Mumbai. "If you have any brains left, you will get on this flight. It's your last chance to get to a criminal-friendly environment before they extradite you to Singapore, and believe me, you don't want that! It's a one-way ticket because you won't need a return portion for quite a while," she added regretfully.

"And where does Miryam fit into all this?" I asked, almost afraid to find out.

Aishe looked at me blankly as if she had no idea what I was talking about.

PART II
STEVE HUNTER

CHAPTER SIXTEEN

The sun had just risen but the sidewalks were already melting. *October 1, 2008,* early fall everywhere else in the world, but in Singapore it was a same-same equatorial day as every other day of the year. Hot and muggy. Steve Hunter luxuriated in the air-conditioned comfort of his fully-equipped bachelor pad, taking his time getting out of bed. No reason to hurry. All of the world's major exchanges were in earlier time zones and firmly shut down. Except for the Nikkei, but he had steered clear of it post-Kyoto-quake. "That whole country is in a quake zone. Kyoto might very well happen again, only next time it will be Tokyo," he had been told at Harvard.

He didn't have much love for Singapore–its cheerless citizens, its big-brother government–but it was where the Bank had assigned him. Oddly, he related to the city in a visceral way. It, like himself, had risen out of the swamp to become a world player. Who could have imagined that this equatorial hot-house, permanently draped in haze and deadly insects would one day turn into a global financial hub; similarly, who could have imagined that little Stevie, the fifth unwanted child of Texan trailer-home scum, would manage to put himself through university, uncover a facility with foreign languages and display the kind of business acumen it takes to become a Master of the Universe, earning in the seven figures at the unripe age of thirty-two.

In any case, he had very little to do with Singapore and its vicious little quirks. His world played itself out in limousines that drove him from his perfect apartment to an anonymous bank building, where, from a corner office of the top floor, he spent exciting days making huge investments while lazily looking out at sea and the southern tip of Malaysia. And when he needed refreshment or a bit of female company, he had any one of singularly western-style, unaffordable-by-ordinary-folk restaurants and ritzy hotel lobbies. Yes, he had a good life, and his only desire was that it last forever and he would never to have to look back.

His morning routine was fashioned after Jeremy Irons playing Charles Swann in the boring *Swann's Way*, the film that had given him the peeks he needed to claim Proust as his favourite author. Unlike Swann, Steve performed his morning rituals somewhat speedily but, more to the point, on his own, without a valet that he could easily afford. Steve needed to be alone in the morning because he was nurturing a deception.

To start, he gulped down ice-cold mandarin-orange juice which he had squeezed before going to bed. The sweet acidity of his preferred citrus easing his cigarette-rough mouth into wakefulness, he pressed a button that drew back the curtains of his wraparound eighth floor windows to afford him a view of what had remained of "old" Singapore's Chinese-Victoriana, now surrounded by the steel and glass of the jet-age. He stood naked and heroic, with arms outstretched, Wagnerian chords of his own imagining bouncing in his ears, like a champion-warrior of the realm in charge of protecting the domain. He had intentionally chosen this unit over others on higher floors because "eight" is considered lucky by the Chinese and even more because it offered the best possible angle of this dynamically evolving cityscape. It seemed like the skyscrapers were rapidly mutating to encroach and expropriate any of the invaluable real estate at their feet as soon as it was deemed under-utilized and therefore helpless when surrendered to the mercy of Progress.

He touched a button and the coffee which he had also prepped from the night before, started burping and percolating in its Italian gadget. The life affirming wafts signified stage two of his routine.

He threw on a Malaysian *lungi,* its Moslem crisscross design geometrically wrapping his fit body, helped himself to a full cup of the freshly brewed, lit a cigarette and sat down at his desk, set against a wall and away from the view so he could better concentrate on the contents of the computer screen.

The obvious opening salvo: a quick review of the final figures from the Turkish and Indian indexes. Yes, yesterday had indeed been a top-tier day for Steve. A cool million sterling for the bank and another solid contribution to his early retirement and that cute little French chateau he had fallen in love with. Wonderful treats were awaiting in store, and all he needed to achieve them was concentration and confidence that his winning streak would continue unabated. Wishful thinking and unwavering ambition were the tools of his trade, and he believed in bolstering them by daily meditations and shameless fantasies of the untold wealth it was in his power to earn. He always chased these daydreams down with a gulp of good coffee and a strong puff on his first-of-the-day cigarette. It helped.

The second puff on the cigarette was his most important. It was that particular rush of nicotine that helped to dissuade misgivings that he felt at the start of every trading day. It could not be denied. He was unwaveringly and determinedly breaking the most solemn rule of investment banking: he was trading not for clients of the bank as he was meant to, but directly for the bank, with fictitious clients' accounts to cover his tracks. He was doing this to realize maximum profits for the bank and therefore himself. If this practice were ever to surface, he would be fired on the spot and disowned by the entire banking system. He kept at it, because he knew that the bank would never run an audit on him and jeopardize the wonderful pots of money that he was generating, unless there was a serious downturn, a highly unlikely event, considering the savvy with which he was operating.

He switched his attention to his email. Eight messages from the eight women who had shown an interest in him in the last month. Wanting to see him. He also wanted to see them, all of them, but it had been getting more and more difficult to shoo anyone away after sex on lame excuses like "the painters are coming first thing in the morning" or "the plumbers" or "the electricians." It was inconceivable to have anyone stay the night and wake up with him, but his excuses were sounding a bit stale even to himself, as if he was occupying the only dysfunctional state-of-the-art apartment in all of South-East Asia. No, it was better to wait until Istanbul and Bombay.

The email that did excite him was a single-word message from his contact in Turkey. It said, "syntax!" Using Steve's own code it read KalKom: "syn" being Greek for the Latin "com" (with) and "tex" which normally stood for "Texas" but meant California or "cal," then a transposition of the syllables, and a transliteration of the "c's" to "k's" to give the Turkish pronunciation, and *voilà* the name of a big Izmir-based cybernetic company that had for a while been in negotiations to merge with a telecommunications giant. The message meant that the merger was imminent and it was time to start buying!

He put in a pre-order with Istanbul-MKB for a million shares (five million sterling) and turned off the computer as he threw off the *lungi* and headed to the shower. He lathered his body aromatically with an herbal formula from Provence and briefly rinsed with the multiple jets of exactly 90°F water. He turned on the overhead jet and put his head under it. He shampooed and carefully conditioned his hair. All day long it would have to live and sweat in darkness under a wig; he believed in catering to it in the morning.

Warm breezes from several directions dried him off in front of the mirror. Steve admired his own image. Gently toned muscles, not an ounce to spare but not at all skinny, short but full hair with its naturally golden highlights and the hinted waviness it would achieve if allowed to grow longer, striking blue-grey eyes and excellent endowments down-south. "You gorgeous dude, you," he muttered as he did to himself at the start of every day.

He proceeded to take away the most noticeable of the gorgeous-nesses, starting with the eyes. He fitted-in the contacts with the same regret he always felt because he had never gotten used to them. His eyes were now a light undistinguished brown, having been gradually darkened with a series of tinted lenses he had bought at the best optics store of Mumbai during the previous year. No one had been able to pinpoint how and when Steve's eyes had turned brown, nor did anyone remember that they ever were not. Same with the hair.

Steve pressed a secret button and a hidden shelf popped open. He reached in and took out the ensemble of his wig. It had the same colour hair as his own, but corporate length, drably dressed and decidedly thinning, not like his own hair at all. This wig was also the end product of a year's worth of gradually balding versions. The progression of wigs for which he had paid serious money in Istanbul had culminated in a bald spot on the pate and a receding hairline that had to be camouflaged with a comb-over, which had been cleverly designed to hide the forehead seam of the wig. It also gave him the slightly comical look of the vain efforts of all balding men trying to hide the fact. He then put on the zero-prescription, lightly tinted glasses and, presto, a totally different person was staring back from the mirror. This was the Steve everyone in Singapore knew.

He remained nude, except for the contacts and the glasses and the wig, as he fetched his breakfast. Every day the same, muesli with skimmed milk and a dollop of unnecessarily chilled thick Greek honey, alongside a large slice of ideally ripe papaya with a major squirt of lemon and about a teaspoon of chilies as he had learned to do back in Texas via Mexico. He permitted himself a discreet burp and refilled his coffee cup while lighting his second cigarette, not as delicious as the first but essential for the full wake-up.

He opened his closet door and admired the row of identical, absolutely immaculate shirts arranged in diminishing tones of off-white, ironed to a crisp; the many hand-stitched, traditionally-cut suits in barely distinguishable variations of dark-blue, also arranged according to their colour palette; a collection of French silk "power" ties in striking blues and reds; stacks of silk underpants; hillocks of finest quality socks; Italian shoes, all black: the wardrobe of the mighty.

He slipped on the silks and fished out a belly-padded vest from a secret compartment, which he wore as an undershirt. He chose a shirt and a suit at random (all the items went with each other unerringly). Dressing himself quickly but unhurriedly, he made a mental note to give Kim, his "daily," a good bonus for the upcoming Chinese New Year for keeping his apartment and his clothes in such excellent order, but remind her yet again to quit putting the honey away in the fridge and turning it to impenetrable jelly. He put on the socks and shoes and perused himself in the full-length mirror as he adjusted the knot of the day's preferred tie, a sapphire with a single crimson diagonal line. The proper tie is essential for success. This morning's choice was meant to dazzle the big shot from London head-office coming to see him first thing.

He slipped on the suit-jacket and he was ready for his public. Slightly pudgy around the belly and perfectly nondescript otherwise. He saluted his image in the mirror. "You balding, fat, *ordinary* son of a bitch," he thought to himself, as he did every morning after his changeover. "Go get 'em, tiger. Let's show 'em how we do things in Texas!"

CHAPTER SEVENTEEN

"May I come in?" asked Reginald Sunderland as Steve jumped to his feet to welcome him into his office. "Reg" as he was known–and happily not something absurd like "Sunny" or "Sundy"–was the most traveled of all the senior executives of the Bank. It was his job to regularly visit the regional offices and have a chat with the traders in each one, not that they needed much chatting since they had been vetted thoroughly before being placed, and all of them, in particular Steve, had proven themselves many times over with smart trading that was keeping the Bank afloat.

In Reg's mind, it never hurt to infuse them with a bit of London air, a quick visit, some obligatory advice, a bit of prodding in the right direction (the Bank's, not their own) and in times of financial downturns like today's, some cautionary leadership. It was well known that a proper trader could make more money in rough times than good, but the current situation was ominous to say the least.

Reg sat down facing Steve and the extensive view from the windows behind the desk. He ran his hands through his plentiful silver hair and clucked disapprovingly at Steve.

"Looks like you're rapidly losing hair, Stevie-boy. You must stop worrying. You're doing very, very well. It's no secret that the hundred and fifty you generated for us last year was close to thirty percent of our annual profit. We're all very proud of you."

"It's the genes," explained Steve. "Dad was completely bald by forty and mom wasn't far behind," with a chuckle.

"And the belly? Is that congenital too?" chuckled Reg right back, letting his jacket flaps fall open and pushed his purple tie to the side to reveal some of his ultra-trim fifty-five year-old physique.

"That, sir, is the addictive little spring rolls they give away with cocktails at the Mandarin Oriental," admitted Steve.

"The cocktails don't help either, my boy. Stick to single-malt. It'll get you drunk but will not smell on your breath and it's low on calories."

"Would you like a pick-me-up?" asked Steve, taking the hint. He retrieved a bottle of private stock from Aberdeen, Reg's favourite and untouched since his last visit three months ago. Two gleaming tumblers and a bowl of ice-cubes appeared on a side-shelf at the touch of a button.

"A bit early, but why not, and neat, please, no diluters," shrugged Reg, his standard-issue reply.

Whisky in hand, Reg peered at Steve knowingly. "As you might have heard, we are enjoying the last vestiges of calm before what could end up becoming the worst financial climate in recent memory. It is my job to come all this way–bloody terrible the Concord snuffed out, but thank goodness for the flat bed and the tiny shower of first class–and tell you, nay, *order* you to ease up, almost *cease* all trading except for petrol, gold and 'breakfast' futures. And your job is to disobey me, discreetly, and prove everyone wrong by continuing your splendid unearthing of Indian and Turkish gems with which to make yourself, let alone the Bank, some 'real bucks' as you Yanks are fond of saying."

"I promise to be extra careful," answered Steve earnestly, brushing his tongue on the Scotch, not really sipping it at all.

Reg wasn't quite so abstemious. He took a generous gulp and suppressed a small hiccup before continuing. "Head office has suspended all trading, even oil. Now we are busily buying minor-EU-member discounted debt, which will only pay back in a few years, but it is the one sure thing in a very muddled horizon. Particularly so because we are insuring the purchases. Of course, we are also investing on an inevitability: the inexorable multiple defaults of all the sunnier European countries."

"Very wise," agreed Steve. "Greece, Portugal, Italy, Spain, even not-so-sunny Ireland. They're all heading straight into the sewer."

"Wise, yes. Kind, not really. Betting on human misery has never been my favourite game, but one has to make a living." Reg allowed himself his one-second of banker's regret before he returned to form with a magnanimous gesture of self-forgiveness. "Well, if not us, it'll be the Arabs or the Russians or the Chinese, and they would be much harsher than us on our forever drunk, terminally insolvent, incurably corrupt, naughtily spendthrift European-fringe brethren, wouldn't they?"

"Much," agreed Steve, wetting his tongue in his drink by way of encouraging Reg to finish his and leave him alone. Reg followed suit halfway by promptly downing the rest of the whisky in a single draft, but he wasn't quite ready to leave anyone alone yet.

"I have a blessing in disguise for you, Steve," began Reg, clearing his throat, which for him signified a change of subject to the real issue of the meeting. "As you know our loyal and wonderful Francis, your best friend and *settler* of your accounts, the man who has given you all the latitude you need to conduct business while affording you total peace of mind by dealing with London for you, has decided to resign after forty selfless years at the service of the Bank. We disagree that he should leave us, he is after all only seventy-three and has another good ten years at least, but his self-lessness is apparently at an end. He wants to return to his Suffolk home in Twee-on-the-Pring, a dead-end village if I ever saw one, and devote himself to growing horseradish, as painful a crop as ever invented. Somehow I feel at this point he'd be happy to be doing anything at all other than continuing in this office. He is adamant and we have no choice." Reg extended his glass for a refill before continuing. "The short of it is that we have deemed it unnecessary to replace him. His only job the last several years during which you have been with us has been to settle *your* trading accounts and nothing else. Well, you're a big boy and we think you should settle your own accounts from now on. We will pay you ten thousand extra a year for doing it, save the Bank a few times that amount by not having to hire a replacement for Frank, and give you all the liberty you need. What do you say?" Reg raised his eyebrows in a way that allowed for no dissent to this decision.

Steve was taken by surprise. This was not only unusual and against normal banking procedures, it defied all manner of safeguards considering how much hard currency was involved. It would add much unnecessary paperwork to his life, but also allow him almost unlimited license to act on his own and hopefully make some additional cash for himself by making more daring trades. He nodded his assent without reservation.

"Well, my boy," Reg said as he downed his drink, stood up and extended his hand to Steve, all in one fluid motion. "Keep up the good work and try to exercise just a tad of restraint, will you? And, please ease off on the spring rolls. For the sake of your silhouette."

"I promise on all counts," repeated Steve, even more convincingly than the first time.

"Must catch my flight to Hong Kong," said Reg as he quickly shook Steve's hand and deftly exited leaving behind a faint odor of a very expensive man's cologne from a two-hundred year old English cosmetics firm. Lavender mainly, with a hint of magnolia.

Steve got up from his chair and turned to stand in front of his office's wall of windows. Unlike the view from his apartment, here all he could see was a vast expanse of grey-murky sea with a nipple of Malaysia in one corner. He stretched himself to his full height and broke out in a huge smile. The bank trusted him unreservedly.

They had removed all controls on his activities. Well, he would prove even more worthy of their trust than ever. He would continue making them a bundle while adding to his own stash. Once it reached ten million (it was already more than three) he would set out on that hazy sea and never walk into another bank except to use the ATM.

Reinforced by his reverie, he sat back down in front of his computer. Now, he had to play the waiting game. The Istanbul exchange was still two and a half hours away from opening. Steve's only real work on this day was to follow KalKom and to invest another chunk of change into it before the merger was announced. He had to wait past the upheaval of his million-share pre-opening purchase, let the price settle down, and buy another million shares before the announcement. It meant waiting until two o'clock local time for Istanbul to open and then practice his nerves of steel while waiting for just the right moment to reinvest in the next two to three hours after that. Those three pulsating hours of stalking and getting ready to pounce were the surge of excitement for which he lived. They would pass in a flash. It was the next two and a half hours from now that would be slow torment, like trying to get honey to pour out of a jar that Kim had put away in the fridge by habit. In Singapore one puts all foodstuffs in the refuge of the fridge to protect from the heat and the persistent insects, *except* Greek honey that turns solid even if slightly chilled. "Must make a big point of the honey before I give her the bonus," noted Steve to himself, as he accessed the Mumbai and Delhi exchanges simultaneously.

His vast portfolio in the Subcontinent offered no surprises on this day. He had already triumphed there last month when he had smelt out a humongous foreign investment in a local farm machinery outfit and bought-in minutes before the rumour became fact. He had made a tidy four million quid on that, but since then he had had to sit tight on his Indian trading. Those Indians, ever cautious and most seasoned of the planet's traders, were taking no chances these days of impending financial Armageddon. His portfolio of holdings valued at half a billion pounds had budged by an averaged fluctuation of one-point-four percent. Not terrible but nothing to cheer about.

Steve signed out of his computer and headed for an early lunch. It was eleven thirty, still a full hour and a half away from the opening bell in Istanbul and the start of fun & games.

The Singaporean bar most preferred by bankers, investors, financiers and wannabes was across the sweltering street from the Bank. Steve athletically by-passed the air-conditioned tunnel that the Bank had funded to save sweat spots on the suits of employees crossing the street, walking to the bar on the surface. He enjoyed a few minutes of exposure to the oppressive, anvil-like sensation of the city's climate; it reminded him of all the pressure and unbearable discomforts he would be facing if he ever screwed up and lost his job. His was the kind of job that can only be lost for misconduct, and once so branded impossible to recover.

The bar was a detailed replica of an English pub, with little nooks for conspiratorial privacy, every brand of UK beer and ale, and a buffet brimming with unhealthy, meticulously authentic English bar-snacks. It was an irresistible banquet for homesick Brit (and by association, American) financial wizards to enjoy a Scotch egg and a pint while fishing for information from fellow sufferers.

Moments after Steve had entered the bar he was accosted by his "shadow," Brett, a fellow Texan—in fact the only other Texan working in the city—a recent arrival who had latched onto Steve for all manner of support in the name of their shared State of provenance. Steve, who wanted nothing ever more to do with Texas, and who on principle refused to ever befriend a fellow trader—you never know what little snip of conversation could cost you money–nevertheless responded to Brett because he found him amusing. He had helped him with neutral concerns, most urgent of which was to meet women, and used him as a shield against other traders by sitting with him and having long, seemingly uninterruptible conversations.

Brett was particularly effusive and grateful this day. He had finally maneuvered into bed a Swiss banker to whom Steve had introduced him, and it had been really "hot," and not only that but she had given him a nice lead into the Indonesian market, and he didn't even have to fish for it. His entire body seemed to be smiling.

"What do you call a Frenchman with manners?" asked Brett conspiratorially.

"Swiss?" guessed Steve, laughing obligatorily.

"Exactly!" echoed Brett, with a loud chortle. "One of her jokes."

"I can imagine," said Steve as he sipped his ginger-beer. "What else did she tell you?"

"That your 'settler' has quit, and that you're now in charge of your own trading. I'm impressed, Steve, I'm really impressed. That is outstanding, my friend!"

"She told you this last night?"

"At about two a.m."

"I didn't find out until this morning."

"Hey, don't blame me! 'What has more holes than Swiss cheese?' 'The private affairs of a major trader!' Another one of her jokes."

"This woman is a comedic treasure-trove," remarked Steve drily.

"Oh, come on, man! It's great news! And be happy it spread before it even happened. That is usually how *bad* news circulates."

"So, what's the deal with Indonesia."

"Hey, I had to emit bodily fluids before I could get that information."

"Spill it, you bastard! There would have been no emissions if I hadn't helped you out with her."

"Yes, you did me a huge favour.... And I owe you."

"So?"

"I... can't!" Brett was struggling. "Please, Steve. You're a major player. Let me have this little nugget. Please...."

"You're pathetic, and I'm not so sure, a Texan. Stop sniveling and spill the beans. Share! It's the only way to stay on top."

"I thought that was the surest way to sink to the bottom."

"Who told you that?" asked Steve innocently.

"You," Brett said almost inaudibly, as both men burst out laughing.

§

At exactly two p.m. Singapore time (9 a.m. in Istanbul) Steve tuned into his KalKom vigil. The stock stumbled awkwardly at first, rising artificially for the first ten minutes—obviously as a result of Steve's own big purchase—and then slowly declined over the next hour as traders pushed and shoved to sell and make small immediate profits. For a short minute at three-thirty the price dipped below what it had been at yesterday's close but Steve waited it out. No reason to take unnecessary risks; the merger could meltdown at the last moment. His contact in Istanbul, as per their understanding, would email him the most propitious moment to buy more stock.

The email came at three minutes past four. It said simply: "yes." Steve punched in some numbers and purchased another million shares (five point one million sterling) but instinctively he assigned this transaction to "error account," No. 88888888. This was a fully functional and official account of the Bank, but beyond the immediate surface of the Bank's activities. It had originally been set up to "correct" a mistake of his predecessor, some trivial, five thousand quid that had been invested in the wrong stock and which the bank had had to correct without having to spell-out to their own stockholders. It was a device that all banks use to cover their tracks and totally legal since eventually it is included in the accounting records of each year's fiscal reports–under miscellaneous–but a nice little niche to hide in temporarily if an innocent mistake were to occur. No. 88888888 was used only once during all the years that Francis had been settling for Steve and it had been to correct an errant two hundred and fifty pounds that seemed to evade all methods of calculation including the abacus. With Francis now gone, Steve could use the account for what he considered an essential aspect of secrecy. By dealing out of the eight-eights he could stay under the radar of rivals from other banks as well as the sharks within his own Bank. The error account spoke only for itself, it could belong to any private trader, but the transfer between it and the official Bank account was mere flicks of the mouse which he could practice anytime he needed. What he hoped was that KalKom would perform as predicted and suddenly eight-eights would be a very wealthy account indeed. By keeping the money in there, instead of immediately consolidating it with the principal account, he would be able to gather a little "secret" fortune, trade anonymously from it at will and really shock the Bank into admitting his greatness when he presented them with an additional fount of profits at year's end. This might end up being my greatest coup yet, he mused, as he waited for the KalKom miracle to occur. They might name this move after me! "Pulling a Steve" they could call it.

The good news arrived sharp at noon, Istanbul time (5 p.m. in Singapore). The merger was announced, and within minutes the stock shot up to fifteen pounds a share from the five it had been earlier. A two-hundred percent profit. It was bound to rise even more but it's not a banker's job to speculate for small marginal gains when the major gain is in-hand. Steve sold his entire holdings in KalKom, all two million shares, and bagged a profit of ten million sterling into the official Bank account as well as another ten million into the "error" account. A total earning of twenty-million sterling for a single day's performance. A cause for extensive celebration. There were banks who would welcome such a profit on investment over a much longer period, months even.

Steve gave himself a discreet pat on the back and a reward of his single-malt that had been sitting on the desk unfinished since Reg's visit in the morning. He drank it down in one gulp and signed off for the day.

CHAPTER EIGHTEEN

His first order of business once back in the privacy of his apartment was a rigorous hour-long regimen, a workout meant to maintain his fighting trim, a great asset in sexual conquest which he always had to exercise in a hurry during trips away from home-base. He used a couple of pieces of compact equipment, but his routine consisted mostly of stretches and flab-eliminating crunches that he had to fashion by himself from the internet. He would have liked a personal trainer but that would mean exposing a washboard-abdomen instead of the padded-vest pudginess that he showed in public. This would be an exposure that would absolutely compromise his ongoing deception.

To clean off the sweat of the workout he had learned to do without a shower—which would necessitate removal of wig and contact lenses—using instead the Ancient Greek method of olive-oiling himself and scraping grime off with a flat-blade strigil which he had bought in Athens from a salesman who claimed it was a replica of one used in Olympia during the ancient Games. From the same salesman he had ordered a steady supply of Cretan extra-virgin oil scented with essence of orchid that made him smell like an exotic salad, just the aroma to increase his appetite.

Supper this day of immensely satisfying money-making was at the Mandarin Oriental's icily air-conditioned, cavernous main lobby under the tinkling of the twelve-story mobile that seemed to hang in mid-air from the glass roof. The place smelled of success and they made the best Chinese-style fried dumplings in a dumpling-crazed city.

His lawyer, the forever harried ex-New Yorker Joe Schwartz, joined him fifteen minutes late, just in time for the kosher-tolerable chicken *satay*, having gratefully missed the shrimp-laden spring rolls and *har-gow*, which as always Steve would have teased him into trying. He smelled of an entire Singaporean day's worth of spent sweat, a pungent contrast to Steve's olive oil and orchid aroma.

"Ooh, you *steenk*," observed Steve puckering his nose.

"How the fuck do you find time to clean up for dinner, I have no idea," complained Joe. "I work my butt off all day, making sure guys like you are okay, and I end up coming to dinner smelling like a goat. I'm too tired to take a shower even if I had the time."

"Yeah, well, you're doing God's work, Joe. Don't know what I would be without you." Flashing a smile of fake gratitude.

"I also don't know *what*, but I'll tell you *where*! You'd be in jail, my friend, doing hard Singapore time with lashes coming in and lashes going out. Without me to cover your tracks, almost all your transactions would be liable for prosecution, or at least investigation, for insider trading. They can't get you because I will not let them try to prove anything, and because you're smart enough to appear innocent simply by never budging from Singapore. Which makes *me* wonder just how the hell you do discover your dirty little secrets. That Indian farm-machinery business from last month has everyone scratching their heads including your competition, and you know how dangerous it can be to rile the competition!"

"They're just jealous, that's all. Have some more chicken. Lobster-dumplings are next, and as we all know you're *allergic* to sea-food," winked Steve.

"Lobster, is it? What? Are we celebrating?"

"Yup. Caviar is on the way, and champagne, even though I hate the stuff."

"I love it, but with caviar, it has to be ice-cold vodka. They have Bison here, don't they?"

"They have whatever your heart desires."

"That's not really true. They don't have the kind of climate my wife likes, so she refuses to move here. They don't have what my kids love above all else: ice-hockey, and so they will refuse to move here while ice continues to exist on Long Island…. Did I tell you that both the boys earned hockey scholarships, and that yet again I'm going to have to miss all their games–"

"–So should they!" interrupted Steve. "That game is nothing but a sure-fire way to get brain-concussions. You should force them to move here and forget all about hockey–"

"–Well, yeah, *you* try forcing my sons to do anything whatsoever. And, most of all, what they don't have in Singapore is leniency. They have really tough laws and you better stay within them. There is only so much I can do for you if you stray too far."

"Oh, shut up and enjoy, man, and stop spooking me. I just scored big. Real big!"

"That can only be bad news for me. You're already under scrutiny. They'll take out the microscope, I swear to you, and they'll nail you."

"No-o they won't. It's all on the up and up."

"Bullshit, Steve. So, how much?"

"Twenty-million sterling."

"In one day?! You're mad!"

"No, I'm smart."

"No trader is *that* smart. You tapped into your contacts and someone gave you a secret he shouldn't have given you. And even if he did, you weren't allowed to follow up on it. Please remember. You're not some weird billionaire playing the stock market. You are an instrument of a Bank. There are carefully scripted laws, my friend. Whatever you did to make that much money in one day is illegal. Trust me."

"Oh, please. You know I can't deal with real life. Give me a break. You're stressing me out. You're my very expensive lawyer. You're supposed to soothe me."

"Wrong. Get a shrink if you want soothing. Or a hooker. My job is to keep you out of jail. But you need to cooperate."

"I am making tons of money. For both of us. How much more can I cooperate?" Steve gave a dismissive wave of his hand as the silky-glamorous waitress set down the caviar course, including its *blini* and sour cream, beside a freshly opened, ice-covered bottle of perfumed vodka that had arrived from Russia just yesterday.

"Schmuck! The hounds are unleashed. I'm getting the most disturbing possible news out of New York. It's gonna be like an atom bomb and it's coming soon. The entire global market is going to unravel. *Everyone* is going to lose money. And the few that keep making it will be prime suspects for corrupt practices. Especially if they're investing for a bank, and even more especially if they're doing it out of squeaky-clean Singapore. Do you follow me? Take it easy. Lie low! That's an order. In case you haven't noticed, they're very strict here. If you screw around, I won't be able to save you, not even with my high-maintenance little snitch in Justice."

"I promise to be a good boy, okay? Now you quit being such a bully and enjoy your caviar! Okay? Let's pretend we're in the Russian Tea Room and we just got rave reviews for a show we produced on Broadway."

"Oh, why not," grumbled Joe as he spooned about a hundred dollars' worth of *asetra* onto a *blini* and stuffed it into his willing mouth.

§

Steve was much more shaken by Joe's admonitions than he would ever let on. Always wary about any entanglements with the law of that fierce little island-nation, he didn't really need the fires of his fears further fueled with repeated warnings. There was no question in his mind that he would clear out of Singapore the moment things got too hot to handle. He was ready for that in every way he needed to be. However, beyond the intolerable threat of doing time in equatorial dungeons, now he had to face the possibility of an economic downturn (*global* yet) that would make him ever more dependent on access to illegal information if he were to stay on-schedule for his rich and early retirement.

Finally finished for the day, he returned to his apartment exhausted. By the time he had triple-locked his door, taken wig, contact lenses and padded vest off and properly put them away, and smoked his final cigarette of the day, all he felt capable of was to shuck off his clothes and go to bed. No cucumber facial, no almond-oil rub, no turmeric drink, just sleep and some epic soul-searching.

First came the remembrances of Texas. The tight little trailer home, sleeping on top of older, equally unhappy, foul-smelling siblings, as the night mercury reached ninety-eight and the air-conditioning hadn't worked since his father had last had a job and could afford to run it; and the handout meals from the food bank: loads of farty chili and leaden bologna and the big deal of fried chicken and two Drake's Devil Dogs on his birthday. Then followed a quick, all too quick, collage of scholarships and Harvard and rapidly escalating jobs, first in New York and London and then on the international scene. The whole lot melting into a future tableau of rural bliss, a bit like Marie Antoinette's Petit Trianon fantasy-house, where he is dressed as an aristocrat-farmer musically supervising the choreographed harvest of his grapevines to playful Mozartian chords. A joyous scene that soon enough turns ulcerous and peels off the frame to be replaced by a repulsive image of himself chained to a slimy floor in a dark-rank jail cell with the same ninety eight degrees and the same lack of air-conditioning.

This was more or less the content of all his dreams for the longest time. It wasn't a nightly occurrence–he normally slept uneventfully–but regular, about once every six weeks, coincidentally, right after his scheduled meetings with Joe, the lawyer. The ominous message of the shattering endings should have by all accounts been shaking his very core, scarring him with premonitions, injuring his ambition, destroying his ability to stay on course. At least, that would have been the case if Steve was an ordinary financial wizard. If, for example, he had been from a wealthy family and making money was like a game for him and not a do-or-return-to-the-trailer-home as in his case. The nightmare ending of a dream that should be terrifying to him, in reality appeased him. As if the possible disasters had already taken place within it and left him unscathed in real life. Upon awakening he stretched luxuriously in the shadow of the worst scenes of the dream and the sheer terror of its message, because he had decided there was absolution in it and license to continue.

He went through the quasi-Proustian morning ritual with his normal optimism, humming *I did it M-y-y Way* which the Mandarin's dinnertime sound-system had played in three versions (Elvis's, Frank's, and an instrumental for a Karaoke that six idiots had performed abominably). It was a catchy tune, and gave validation to the consistently risky, somewhat immoral career-maneuvers of the Mandarin's regular customers. Steve hummed it during his perusal of the markets–Kalkom had closed for the day exactly where he had sold it hours earlier than that, pleasing him no end–and continued to hum it reading his emails–including the single punctuation mark (!) message from his contact in Turkey–his shower, his transformation into a prematurely aging, typical bank employee, his breakfast with the yet-again solidly chilled honey–*must* speak to Kim–and finally the ceremonial donning of the fat-prosthetic, and correct shirt-suit-tie. Fears and disaster scenarios firmly on-hold, he was now ready to enter the fray for yet another day, but he felt he should pass by Xanthippi's just to make sure.

Xanthippi, or Madame X as she preferred to be called, was an ex-pat, an Istanbul-born Greek, who had originally moved to Singapore with her husband Socrates, an adventurer who loved the Orient and thought he could sell olive oil to the Brit-style Chinese in the pre global-cuisine sixties. He had failed and was murdered in a gambling hole in Kuala Lumpur when he had traveled there to play poker with serious ruffians and had been caught cheating. Left to her own devices and broke, X had become solvent–albeit, modestly–by admitting clients into her humble apartment to exercise her one marketable trade: reading fortunes on Turkish coffee-grounds for those curious or queasy about the future. She had correctly "seen" a totally unpredictable wedding and successfully warned a couple not to travel on a specific day, when the plane they would have taken crashed, killing everyone on board. She had become a legend because of those two instances–whose enormity she had never again matched–and reigned ever since as the highly superstitious city's foremost medium.

Everyone who was anyone wanted to consult her, but she was getting old and accepted very few clients. She refused to accept money officially, seeing it as an evil. Her visitors knew to bring her small presents and discreetly to leave some cash before leaving, a decidedly non-capitalist way to conduct business, much admired in a city that devoted itself to capitalism.

Steve had become one of her favourites as he spoke passable Greek and Turkish and knew Istanbul well, reminding her of her long-lost home. He called on her regularly because he admired her spunk–and also because it was a status symbol to be seen by her–than for any useful advice she had ever given him.

He showed up with the mandatory, pricey coffee-cake in hand. Xanthippi reacted with her prescribed fuss, kissing Steve on both cheeks and exclaiming volubly that he needn't have bothered. She undid the cake's wrapping and slipped it onto a waiting crystal cake-stand, while she cried out appreciatively, exactly as she had done every other time he had come bearing exactly the same cake, purchased from the only pastry-shop of which she was known to approve.

He settled back on the "client" chair that had entertained the buttocks of the high and mighty and they chatted about Moda, the floral Istanbul suburb where she had lived, and the ruby-red tea they could be sipping there by the seaside on this balmy Autumn day instead of broiling in Singapore, as she slow cooked his Turkish coffee on a little portable burner using aromatic coffee ideally roasted to light brown and stone-ground to powder, imported from back home. She poured out a little into the antique Ottoman cup after the first mini-boil and let the rest boil slightly longer, to cook the grounds fully and encourage them to settle completely to the bottom of the cup. She topped up the cup and brought it to him, with a *lokum* on the rim of the saucer to sweeten the upcoming reading.

Steve sipped noisily, as befits well-turned Turkish coffee, smoking a cigarette. She supervised his drinking and bade him stop before he had drained all the liquid. He then swirled the leftover liquid marrying it to the settled grounds and, using the saucer as a base, he turned the cup upside down. This emptied the grounds onto the saucer, leaving streaks and markings on the walls of the cup, hieroglyphs which a trained fortune-teller knew how to "read."

She studied the cup longer than usual. She shook her head and looked at him smiling. She spoke to him in Greek:

"Well, my Stéfane, it won't be long now. You will meet the woman of your life. And, no, no. Don't laugh at me. I know you meet a new 'woman of your life' every day, but this one is special. And of course, there will be complications. But, later on. You'll have to come back to me for those. Right now, your cup is full of closeness, of, dare I say it, *love,* certainly *romance.* And, she is not from here. She is from somewhere far, and she lives in a place that is even farther. She dominates your cup, nothing else seems important." She stopped meaningfully and peered at the cup again, turning it this way and that. "Of course, I see many, many problems at your work, but it doesn't take a cup to know there are problems ahead for people like you. It takes knowing what you do and reading the newspapers. I will therefore not bother you with any of that. As you know, Steve, the woman is everything." She looked at the cup one final time. "And yes, you are going traveling, but that I see every time." She poured the grounds from the saucer into the cup and read the residues that were left on the saucer. "Amazing," she said. "The same woman on the saucer! Though… there will be a huge problem down the line. Be careful!" She poured a little water into the cup and swirled it around, as a way of sealing his fortune. She deposited the cup upside on the saucer. She bowed her head to indicate the end of her reading. He placed a hundred-dollar bill discreetly under the plate of the coffee cake and kissed her goodbye.

CHAPTER NINETEEN

Steve spent a listless day at the office. His twin Istanbul/Mumbai markets-of-interest offered little in the way of action. It was almost as if both institutions were "on hold" waiting out the period before the promised crisis that was certain to erupt within this very October. It was obviously time for another of Steve's "research" trips.

He needed a new nugget to look forward to. The Kalkom payoff had taken more than three months of close pursuit to flower as well as it did. It had budded in a stray strand of conversation at a promotional party for celebrity-designed beach-slippers at an Istanbul hotel, and he had Hussein follow it doggedly for him all the way to its twenty-million sterling bonanza. Yes, it was time for a little tour. Mumbai first, as always the Yacht Club and Hutoshi, and Istanbul from there. A hefty cash reward to Hussein who had done such a skillful job chasing down the exact timing for Kalkom. And possibly to meet the woman Xanthippi had seen in the coffee cup. He didn't much believe in fortune-telling, but one never knew, did one?

He announced his plans for a week-long absence from the office (to *regenerate* at a spa in Bali) and rang Aishe in Istanbul to organize his trip. He packed his alternate wardrobe and was on an airplane the same afternoon. Air Singapore first class to Mumbai, looking absolutely spiffy and trim, his blue-grey eyes sparklingly free of the contact lenses, his full head of short hair with its golden streaks so very grateful to come out of hiding from beneath that stupid wig, and a counterfeit passport identifying him as Jefferson Cooper, a Canadian. He drank a silent champagne toast to Joe, chasing down delicate lobster tempura that his lawyer's religiosity would not allow–Steve who grew up without ever tasting a delicacy would never be able to grasp how anyone could forego such succulence for any reason whatsoever.

He was aware that traveling under a fake name with a fake passport that was concocted by some underground outfit in Marseilles and then found its way to Istanbul where he had bought it, was illegal even if he were not a bonded trader of a reputable bank. The fact that he had carefully disguised himself so that his true appearance could pass as this fake person, complete with a credit card and other documentation bearing the fake name, could in court be used to prove far-reaching premeditation and was probably punishable with quite a few lashes if convicted in Singapore. He was, however, not bothered. He felt immune from punishment because his reason for the elaborate deception was not meant to buck the law but to give him license to penetrate the business worlds of India and Turkey without the restrictions of his official status. Just a playboy investor with an appetite for some forgiveable insider information. Only marginally illegal and rarely prosecuted; unethical? Oh, God, yes.

Ethics was a luxury where he hailed from, as rare as lobster. Survival was everything.

§

The likable but tight-lipped Arvind Singh was there to fetch him at the airport, once again denying that anyone had organized the pick-up, claiming instead that he had made a reservation for this date last time he had visited. Steve did not contradict him. He loved the Yacht Club and they loved him. They would never admit that they needed anyone to tell them how well to treat him since they had made him their own, elevating his status to Master Yachtsman even though Steve hated sailing as it made him nauseous. It had to have something to do with his hundred-dollar-bill filled deep pockets, but even overpaid, the Club was still cheaper than a four-star, and it had its Tea Room and Bar where *tout*-Bombay came to drink real English tea and alcohol, to kibitz and share secrets.

Akhbar, Arvind's father and manager of the Yacht Club, as effusively welcoming as ever, helped him settle in, but Steve had no time to linger. His libido dictated that he shower and change into his white linen suit and lavender silk shirt–a diametrically opposed style to the darkness of his outfits in Singapore–and repair to Mumbai-girlfriend Hutoshi's artistic-haven apartment in neighbouring Coloba.

She did open the door for him after several minutes of knocking and three promptings on the cell phone, but she warned him that she was in no mood for him. Her recent show of paintings, on which she had laboured for three years and spent all her money, had fizzled out without a single mention in the media and zero sales. She was devastated. Now utterly broke and unhappy, she was busily considering suicide, and punishing herself with a neglect that was somehow defeating her timeless Pharsee beauty and all of her normally formidable sex appeal.

Steve tried to soothe her with a hug for the sake of all the sexually supercharged moments of their past, but had to withdraw as she had obviously not showered for days and stank like fermented garlic. He twitched his nose and she noticed.

"How like you," she said accusingly. "Here I am on the doorstep of the poorhouse, or... *worse,* I can't even pay my rent, damn it! And all you can think of is that I smell. You are incurably petty, Jefferson!"

Steve took out a stack of hundred-dollar bills and laid them on the table. "That is for your rent. Now take a shower, get pretty and let's go out for dinner."

"Right! Then come back here so that you can screw me to your heart's content."

"Only if you want me to, and judging from our many wonderful–"

"–well, you can forget all about those wonderful *whateverses*. That was before. Now, sex is the last thing on my mind, and much worse since you are giving me money, I'd feel like a good-old whore!"

"I can take the money back if it offends you."

"It offends me to the core, but I need it. Leave the money where you put it, but get out of my house."

"I can't leave you like this."

"I'll be alright. Call me next time you're in town."

"I could never forgive myself if you did something stupid."

"I'll be alright. I need time, that is all. And your money. That helps. Now, please leave. Go, go, go!"

Steve wandered the youthful streets of Coloba in great distress. Hutoshi's despair, and even more so her steely rejection, had aroused him immeasurably. He had no problem controlling himself in Singapore, but once in his hunting grounds of Bombay and Istanbul, his semen overflowed, so to speak. He considered masturbation but decided to delay that solitary, rather undergraduate pleasure since a visit to the Yacht Club's Tea Room would be enough to soothe him for now.

He sat beside the oldest of the Tea Room habitués, the venerable Vijendra Vaadaspati, known as VV, who had given up enormous wealth to become a monk in a Rishikesh ashram when he was sixty, and had returned to the marketplace at eighty, penniless but famous enough to trade on credit. He had built another huge fortune in less than three years. Now, seven years hence at the age of ninety, he was among Bombay's richest for the second time in his life. His knowledge of India's business was so comprehensive that he was said to be capable of squeezing gold even out of cow patties.

"Oh, the dashing Master Yachtsman himself, Mister Jefferson Cooper," he said half-opening his eyes. "And to what do we owe the pleasure?"

"I missed having tea with you, so I rushed back, VV," smiled Steve.

"You did well. I've been very anxious to give you an important trading tip. It can be invaluable if you follow it to the letter."

Steve was taken by surprise. VV had not gotten where he was by giving tips of any kind to anyone. "What is it, if I may ask?"

"I'll spell it for you: dee-oh-en-apostrophe-tee. *Don't!* You'll regret it."

"That bad, huh?"

"Worse, really. Cobwebs have taken over the Stock Exchange. Nothing has moved there in ten days, except for Mr Parawhati's bowels which have been purging at will because his wife had to go to Thiruvananthapuram for her father's funeral, and he was obliged to eat in restaurants." VV laughed at his own joke.

"And all because the end of the world is coming?"

"In a nutshell, Mister Cooper."

"A-ah Mister VV, a predator knows where to find game in a famine and water in a drought. I believe that you are living-breathing proof of that."

"I'm guessing that you speak from experience, sir, though all of us are still amazed that you conduct business so very successfully in total secrecy. I mean, you are successful, are you not?"

"Not in your league, sir, not even close."

"Even I am no longer in my own league. This famine and this drought, and all the upcoming repercussions that are poised over our heads like daggers.... I don't know. I fear that big and scary moments are ahead. The prey is about to turn on the hunter and neither will survive."

"Does that mean you aren't making much money these days?" asked Steve mischievously.

The tea service had arrived. Lapsang with hot milk and double sandwiches for Steve. Darjeeling and *chewda* for VV. Both men nibbled and sipped in silence for several minutes.

"I've been losing quite a bit of money actually," VV finally conceded. "Quite a bit."

§

Istanbul was Steve's most articulated refuge. A place, that, as distant from the suburbs of Waco, Texas as is possible, had felt like home to him on first contact. This was his fifteenth visit, a sort of benchmark in view of the Chinese sensitivity to the power of that number. His attachment to Sino-numerology, combined with his inner conviction that it was in Istanbul where he'd meet Xanthippi's "woman from far away" sent a shiver of sexual excitement through him. He had women stashed all over the Imperial City, business-person expats working here, but all of them were tiring him with the detachment and recriminations he deserved for his infrequent and all too brief attentions. He felt no love from any of them, only a reciprocal sexual release by lonely people trapped in a foreign city. However, Steve, despite any indications to the contrary, was a wannabe hopeless-romantic. He yearned for love but knew he was incapable of the sacrifices it required, so he invariably had to settle for sex.

He threw open the garden doors of his ground floor apartment high up the hill in Cihangir, and sent another whispered thank-you to Aishe. He had a panoramic view of the Bosporus as it flowed sapphire-like towards the historicity of Sultan Ahmet and its fifteen hundred years worth of palace sex. Just like Aishe to find him an Istanbul home-away-from-home where articulated sexual memories were as luxuriously in place as the wisteria bordering the French windows, the plush furniture, the tropical-rain shower, the jacuzzi and the always newly decalcified espresso machine for thick, rich coffee *crema*. Not to mention the well-supplied champagne cooler and the quarter-kilo of fresh-from-Odessa *asetra* extra-extra.

He made coffee—using his favourite brand of Italian grounds, as usual awaiting him courtesy of Aishe's comprehensive service—and sipped it with profound contentment in front of his priceless view, being caressed by perfumed Anatolian breezes and the lingering warmth of Istanbul's benign autumn. He accompanied the boost of the caffeine with the voluptuous pink-sweetness of a ripe fig, possibly the last of its kind this season, yet another touch of Aishe's detailed pampering.

His ideal segue to the superlative combination of view, coffee and fig would have been the surprise arrival of a beautiful woman, a young and influential banker, who would regale him with juicy love-making and let him in on some lucrative details of an upcoming market coup. Had Aishe really been on the case, she would have arranged it, he mused naughtily, as he dressed and groomed himself for his lunch with Hussein.

The restaurant of choice for the meetings with his main-man in Istanbul was in the centre-point of Istikilal Caddessi, the pedestrian-and-tramcar-only commercial street between Taxim and Beyoglu, the geographical heart of modern Istanbul. The restaurant was a crowded favourite, where a foreigner dining with a local person was commonplace and whose costly menu offered serious, expertly prepared Ottoman specialties, unlike too many of its opportunistic neighbours with their expedient food and lower prices. He had been here so often, he could find it blindfolded.

Steve took a seat at a table for two. As if by magic, Hussein perched himself on the rim of the empty seat opposite him, his eyes darting from him to the street outside the picture window, his hair, freshly dyed day-glow yellow and sculpted onto his scalp in a heavily lacquered hairdo straight out of a thirties Hollywood film.

"I would sincerely appreciate you not staring at me and buy me lunch instead. I am famished and I'm totally broke, I don't have a gold-coin to my name," he said in Arabic in lieu of hello.

"Do I know you?" asked Steve in mock annoyance.

"How the hell can you know me? How can anyone *know* any-one?" continued Hussein in English, as he settled back in his seat and snapped his fingers impatiently at the waiter.

"I wish you wouldn't do that," countered Steve. "You'll piss him off and he'll spit into our plates."

"A little spit never hurt anyone," he mumbled and turned to the waiter to place the order in Turkish, as usual too fast for Steve to follow and have a say in what they were meant to eat.

"I hope you didn't order the sheep's head again," moaned Steve.

"It's a delicious dish, and one of our greatest national delicacies. You should learn to love it if you intend to continue making for-tunes off our backs," scoffed Hussein. "But no fear. I did not order it." And, just as he said that, the waiter lowered a plate of it with the various meats of the head neatly shaved off and the obligatory eyes placed tastefully in the middle. "He must have brought it by mistake," he shrugged while barking at the waiter to remove it instantly and feed it to his dog.

"How come you're so broke? An enterprising fellow like you?"

"Because I spend all my time making sure *other* people make money, that's why."

"You have a rich father."

"Very, very rich. Most successful investor of this country. The Warren Buffet of Turkey. And the stingiest prick of both shores of the Bosphorus. He refuses to give me a Lira, not a single *kurus*. Nothing."

"He shares his information with you. To encourage you to invest on your own."

"Oh, you Americans! You can be so stupid, eh? He doesn't share anything. I *steal* the information. By hacking his computer, by bugging his phone. And since I have no money with which to *use* the information, I give it to crooks like you, and who knows what you do with it. You don't exactly shower me with money, do you."

"Only when I have to," smiled Steve as he pushed an envelope, fat with fifty one-thousand Turkish Lira notes, across the table.

Hussein quickly scooped up the envelope and shoved it into an inside pocket of his kidskin jacket. It made for a suspicious bulge on his otherwise trim torso. "I hope there is money in there, not just cut-up pieces of newspaper."

"Why don't you take a look."

"It's alright, I trust you."

"How can you? We just met," said Steve without blinking.

"You wouldn't cheat me. You need me. Plus, I'm far too good-looking."

"You *are* good-looking. Especially with the new wig."

"It is *not* a wig! But, seriously, do you like it?" giggling and running his fingers lightly over the coif, like most stylish men when the conversation turns to their new hair-cut.

"If it made you any prettier I'd be chasing you around the table," said Steve earnestly.

"Horny again, are we?"

"Terminally," declared Steve solemnly.

"Then I have just the solution for you. A queen. No, an empress! You'll die when you meet her. You'll kiss my ass for the favor I'll be doing you. But you won't have to. It'll be done because you're a guest in my city and it'll be my pleasure to please you... even as I really need money, but I'm no pimp. No, I couldn't possibly accept money for the introduction, even though… and you'll agree with me when you see her… she's ideal for you in every conceivable way, worth easily ten or twenty thousand Liras! But, no, no, no! I couldn't, I *wouldn't,* ever accept money for such a thing. No, sir! No way–"

"–alright! I heard you. No money, I agree."

"Of course you agree. You're tight as a dead clam when it comes to money. You worship it. You're worse than my father. You're a slave to it. You wouldn't part with a penny if my life depended on it!"

"That's correct," agreed Steve. "So, where is she?"

At that moment a cascade of plates descended on their table. Spicy braised liver and rice-stuffed mussels and grilled sardines and fried fresh-anchovies and marinated tuna and broiled kebabs and charred peppers and stewed green-beans and a spectacular salad of fresh arugula with the reddest tomatoes on the planet. "First we eat, *you* pay, then Varsha," winked Hussein.

§

Desserts on the way, Hussein dialed a number and nervously tapped his fingers until it was picked up. He was brusque: "Get your pretty ass down here. I have someone for you and he's starved, the poor bastard…. Yeah, of course he's handsome. Would I call you if he was not? Also he is rich and, well, he's very, very suitable… Pasha's Table on Istiklal. And hurry!"

Steve had barely licked off the last nibble of his *kazan dibi* pudding, relishing its sweet chicken shreds and caramelized crust, when Varsha arrived swaying as if to a Subcontinental melody on a properly seasoned sitar. She was a bundle of contradictions. Imposing but not tall, full-bodied yet willowy, smooth-skinned and youthful but demonstrably mature with more than four decades of eventful history in every glance of her fiery eyes, a modern woman living alone in Istanbul dressed in a diaphanous black silk sari from her homeland, embroidered with hundreds of tear-like faceted amethysts. A vision of elegance, sparkling like lilacs in springtime.

Hussein stood up and moved out of her way as she lowered herself into his seat. Ignoring him totally, she extended her hand to Steve, while waving her head to resettle richly brown, shoulder-length hair back into the architecture her hairdresser had devised. Steve, grateful to forego the *namaste* he felt certain would have accompanied the sari, touched her hand just long and warmly enough to announce his intentions. Hussein, no longer relevant, simply turned and left to rejoin the parade of the needy on the street.

"You're cute, but I'm here strictly to evaluate you. Don't get any ideas," she warned him. "I'm well off, very independent but also an incurable sentimentalist. I'm impervious to beauty, it's everywhere," she gestured grandly to include the totality of Istanbul's pulchritude. "No, I want to find the unattainable: a real person with some emotions he doesn't mind sharing."

"You smell wonderful," he said.

"A spray of Givenchy accented with a hint of attar of rose. From Lucknow."

"I know Lucknow."

"I don't. I'm from Bombay."

"I was just there. The Yacht Club."

"I didn't know you could get into that place anymore from the cobwebs," she teased. "Your first visit?"

"Bombay is my second home, I love it."

"Really?" she asked, her intended sarcasm lost in a wave of nostalgia.

"Of course, I also love Istanbul," he said to further enhance his likability.

Varsha chortled. She was used to Turkish younger men who would do and say anything at all to get into her pants and her purse, but grown-up anglophones had proven far less accommodating, usually demeaning her into doing all the work. Which is why she generally avoided them. This attractive man, sexually charged and young enough to excite her, was a revelation to her. He was making a sincere effort to seduce her. Without intending to, she reached over and tweaked his cheek, affectionately but forcefully, just a tad painfully like a benign dominatrix. As if he was the son she never had and the ideal younger lover she had despaired of ever finding.

"Sorry," she mumbled withdrawing her hand.

"I had an aunt who used to pinch me like that. I had pink cheeks as a child," he smiled, stroking his cheek.

"I'm not your aunt," she said fixing him with her gaze.

"And I no longer have pink cheeks. I'm a grown man now."

"You'll have to prove that," she whispered naughtily.

"Oh, I'm ready," he said and stood up taking hold of her hand to kiss it. He took her to his apartment.

§

The sex was better than either of them could have hoped for. Uninhibited and intertwining, it flowed from position to position, in sequence, as if each was thoroughly familiar with the other. Heated yet leisurely, with many mutual climaxes. Steve almost as often as Varsha. Passionate but not forceful, exhausting yet exhilarating. It went on for many hours, from late afternoon into evening into night into the first light of dawn until sleep overcame them both, but not before Varsha could moan, "I love you, I want you, forever," something that Steve had always wanted to hear, and here, from this woman, he believed it, he welcomed it.

CHAPTER TWENTY

It had been a precarious time, an eternity of adversity since the heady tryst with Varsha. The predicted market downturn had occurred disastrously right on schedule in late October, and overnight the market had become an unmanageable team of wild horses racing unchecked towards doom.

Steve had lost a fortune trying to tame the inexorable even though he now manipulated his portfolio as if walking on eggshells. Gone the profits he had so craftily accumulated during all those years of savvy and bravado and hard work. The Bank's main account was perilously close to red ink, even after he had transfered into it the ten-million-buffer he had originally stuffed into the 'error-account.' His trading allocation was essentially depleted, his portfolio brimming with items that were being discounted daily as he doggedly held on, praying for a turnaround. He refused to accept defeat. It would be like admitting the end of life as he wished it. It made him panic, and it showed in his behaviour. He was growing irritable and abrupt, shouting and scoffing, as if looking for a fight, a far-cry from the smug-friendly Steve that had ruled the universe.

At first, for more than three weeks, the Bank pretended to be above anything so mundane as an economic burn-out. Aside from a large operating capital, they had centuries' old solid investments in the coffers–worth just north of a billion sterling–and they had been buoyed into their sense of fake security by, of all things, the fictitious black ink of Steve's weekly investment reports. However, none of their other traders were showing a profit and London had been apprised of the worrying shift in Steve's demeanour. They decided to spring for the expensive services of a highly reputed motivator/guru to make a quick tour of their major international branches to bolster morale or at least to instill some fear and caution on the troops.

A steamy late-November morning was chosen for the Singapore *guru-torial,* which all personnel were obligated to attend, particularly Steve, despite his purported crisis-proof success. He tried to weasel out of the event, but to no avail. His superiors would not hear of it, and when Steve continued to demure, he got a phone call from none other than Reg from London, urging him–ordering him–to attend, not only for his own sake but also as a good example for the rest.

The meeting was held in the big reception room, normally reserved for only the most important business–the visit of an oil-sheik to negotiate terms of his investments–but lacking any of the catering of such occasions. This morning there was only nondescript coffee and mealy commercial croissants–in the service of austerity.

Bill, the guru, entered through a side-door, as if reticent to walk through the crowd. He walked briskly to the desk on the podium, and smiled faintly at the traders through dark glasses. Steve despised him on contact. His ludicrous outfit of sneakers and track suit, both of which showed not even a trace of ever having been used for exercise, his arrogant sunglasses, his Hollywood haircut, his supercilious smirk. And then the "stare." An unrelenting gaze through dark lenses right into Steve's soul, agitating him, visibly unnerving him. He felt targeted. As if Bill had been told to single him out for a personal lashing. He opened his mouth, did not introduce himself, and spoke directly to Steve.

"I am going to tell you two stories and stop after each one to hear your reactions." He took a single sip of water. "The first story is about a centipede. You've heard of 'em, right? The deadly little critters that pop up when you least expect 'em, and can kill you if you're not careful?" He took a deep breath, to indicate what?

The seriousness of his topic? "Well, there was this friend of mine, a very nice guy, but a Jain. Kind of full of himself for bein' such a humanitarian and all, never even wantin' to kill an ant, walkin' the streets with a broom, gently sweepin' the ground in front of him to remove any bugs and insects he might otherwise step on. So, he's one of those, okay? And he's walkin' the streets of some Gujarati holy town where he lives and has never traveled from, and he's sweepin' the street as usual, when a huge centipede, some six inches long with really deadly purple pincers on both ends of his ugly body, attaches itself to the twigs of the broom and refuses to be swept away. Our Jain dude is a little confused almost pissed off, though he would never admit it. Jains do not get pissed off, even when they are. He's shakin' the broom and talkin' to the centipede, nice-like, to get his ass off the twigs, but nothin'. That poisonous little viper is there to stay and now he begins to move, slowly mind you, up the handle of the broom, wigglin' and inchin' up using all hundred of his little legs. Comin' awful close to our friend's hands. So, what to do? He can chuck the broom, but then another Jain is likely to find it and lift it up and get bitten; or he can grab the broom from the twig end and hit the handle against a wall to dislodge the centipede, possibly harming the little predator, so he's kinda stuck, right? And what does he do? He reaches for the critter and tries to remove it with his hand. Bi-ig mistake! The centipede bites him and the Jain-man dies after great pain and suffering within three days. His last concern: he asks the nurse if the centipede survived the incident. He is told that his son was so outraged with what happened that he crushed it to death with his shoe. The Jain moans with despair that the incident for which he was responsible had also corrupted his son, as he breathes his last. So what would you have done?" He stretched an elegant hand at Steve, who had fidgeted throughout the recital, and now, singled out for a first response, he felt as if he was being goosed. But not quite humbled:

"I am a little disappointed by your story," he offered with a shrug. "I am not Jain, I eat garlic and onion, I don't hide my houses of worship in forbidden valleys, and I have deadly fear of poisonous crawlies. I would have tried to kill it on first contact. No, I must admit, I can't identify with this... this *dude's* predicament at all. Not at all."

"Still, you're a smart fellow, you can theorize, can't you?"

"Fine. I'll play."

"So, what would you have done?"

"I told you, I'd have killed that damned insect on first sight." Steve waved his hand impatiently.

"Except that killing it is not always the safest option."

"You mean, like the crisis? You can't just kill it and wish it away? You have to deal with it gingerly, because it can turn on you? So what else is new? Is that the best you can do? And why aren't you quizzing someone else? I have nothing to add here."

"You, sir. You're the one who matters. You're the captain of this team. You're the one I want."

"Well, you can't have me!"

"Why not?"

Steve raised his voice a notch: "I have enough on my plate. You can't shove this on my head. I'm not the captain of anything. I'm one of the traders, that's all!"

"But, it's not. Is it? You're not *just* a trader. You are *the* trader of this office. Aren't you?"

"Well, that's none of your business!" screamed Steve.

"I've been paid to make it my business," countered Bill equivocally.

Steve was seething. Instead of continuing to argue, he stood up to leave. Bill held up his hand and took off his sunglasses. "Wait, sir, please. I have another story. You might like it better. You might even just be able to identify with it."

"I doubt it, and it doesn't matter, because I'm doing just fine, thank you." Steve turned to the door.

"Come back and sit down, sir," shouted Bill at his back. "I'm not finished. You're bein' very rude."

Steve turned around in degrees. The assembled held their collective breath. "I am busy and need to return to work," he said patiently.

"Work can wait. I'm tryin' to show you somethin' new. To help you out during what will prove to be a most awful time for your profession."

"You might succeed if you weren't so obvious, so... boring," replied Steve with malice.

"I suggest you stop talking and just sit down!" barked Bill as he replaced the sunglasses on his eyes.

"Fuck off, you stupid jerk," hissed Steve coolly and forged out of the room amid much gasping and some giggles.

§

Steve shut himself in his office, seething. He found no solace in anything, not even his view. His suffering did not last long. Reg's second phone call of the day offered him even less recourse than the first. Steve was expeditiously ordered to take a vacation, immediately, all expenses paid, at least three days, to return only after he had calmed down and regained the dignity with which to be entrusted to continue representing the Bank.

Steve uttered an apology and promised to fly out by the evening. His smile spread across his face when he hung up. A perfect chance to check out Bombay and then Istanbul for some long-overdue Varsha.

CHAPTER TWENTY-ONE

November 26, 2008. A date that everyone alive in Mumbai that day will always remember. Bombs and bullets and blood crushed the mighty city–more of a capital than Delhi; more movies than Hollywood; more people than New York; more power than the rest of India combined–reducing it to ashes and fear and confusion.

Among the millions of terrified citizens, Steve Hunter, in his Jefferson-Cooper alter ego, uneasy but safe inside the Yacht Club, stranded while on the prowl for any snippet of information that would give him a prayer or a lead for a good trade.

Another round of extended shelling resounded from the Taj Hotel next door, obviating any kind of business expectations, let alone free movement. A small but determined gang of militant thugs was inside the hotel, holding this jewel of Mumbai hostage, paralyzing the city, trapping Steve inside a dangerous bubble of injury and death.

This was meant to have been a thirty-six hour stopover in Mumbai on the way to Istanbul and Varsha's welcoming embrace after her barrage of phone calls since their first idyll six weeks ago. It now threatened to stall him indefinitely. Decidedly not how a Bombay-host treats Master Yachtsmen. The Singhs, father and son, swung into action. Akhbar spoke to the army and the police not only to break the cordon but to escort the vehicle in which Arvind would drive Steve to the outside world. Not to the airport, which was effectively shut down, but the train station for the Mumbai-Delhi express, the Indian railroad having been imbued by its British builders never to miss a departure, even in time of war.

§

Delhi was as tightly under martial law as its sister city, but functional and ever so grateful to have been spared the fury of the militants. The car that had picked Steve up at the train station drove along deserted divided avenues, the flowers of the neatly landscaped medians his only company.

Delhi-ites were staying indoors en masse during these anger-fused days, which for Steve had ominous significance. What he had imagined as a respite from the rigours of losing money in Singapore had degenerated into a wartime drama, with a clandestine, police-escorted escape, anonymous overlong train journey in a tiny "private" bedroom, and now a ride through a magnificent ghost town, where he was the only person living (not counting the driver), while all its monuments and ornamented mansions and lush foliage were gloriously intact.

This could either be a good omen, singling him out as a survivor against all odds, or a bad one, signifying a world that had self-destructed and had but to kill him to complete the devastation. The conundrum persisted in tormenting him during check-in to the Intergalactic Palace Hotel where several of its employees would have gladly laid on the marble floor so that he could trample them if they felt it would please him.

He relaxed once inside his fully technological room where everything worked with remote controls and the enormous bed was dressed in feathers inside silky cotton and the windows took in at least half of the capital's most famous sites from up above. The world would have to be as rich as him to be able to afford to enter this hotel and find him to kill him. He was safe here, but also sealed in by the nightly curfew that allowed no one the right to enter or exit after dark. Steve was staying for only one night hoping to be able to fly to Istanbul the next day on a VIP air-ticket that Aishe was juggling for him.

He napped to catch up on sleep he had been unable to enjoy on the train, but a nightmare–in which he was being blown to pieces by misguided shrapnel–played on a loop and finally forced him to open his eyes. He could sleep through a variety of negative dreams but watching himself repeatedly being blown to pieces as collateral damage of yet another Pakistani-Indian skirmish was beyond the limits of his tolerance.

He reasoned that a hotel as expensively westernized as this would be holding some kind of heavyweight party somewhere in its bowels. To properly infiltrate the phantom event he donned his "Jefferson Cooper" business-outfit: a suit of the same colour palette as his more normal Singaporean wear, but stylishly cut by some Italian fashion-guru and closely fitted better to showcase his trim physique; a creamy silk shirt with grey collar; a tie strikingly etched with stripes of various shades of green, just like the hues of money.

He must have guessed right, because seconds after he emerged in the lobby looking lost, a solicitous assistant-manager took him under his care and led him to a very private corner of the night-flower perfumed garden, fetched him a tag on which to write his name and released him on the unsuspecting gathering, all of whom, men and women, were bearing tall glasses of iced alcoholic beverages and were dressed in identical dark-blue suits and whitish shirts, but none with as interesting a tie as Steve's.

Steve could never talk shop with total strangers on an empty stomach. Once fortified, however, he could charm any little or big confidence out of the tightest ass. So, he followed his nose to the overlong buffet that hugged the back-end of the space and was copiously loaded with far too much food, replicas from every cuisine on the planet, except Indian. He piled his plate with a multinational assortment of delicacies whose own aromas were overwhelmed by the sweet smell of the night flowers now directly overhead hidden in the branches of a bush.

"It is unpleasant to eat if one cannot smell the food," laughed an educated voice beside him. It belonged to one of those "world's most interesting men" with the elegantly greying hair and the expensive London-bought clothes, identified simply as "Krishna" on his name tag. "Nasty night-blooming–"

"–primroses?–"

"–no. These are jasmine and just like your primroses they emit their cloying little odour to mask everything. They were put here on purpose, you know. Most of the guests at these parties come here straight from their offices and would smell to high heaven were it not for the flowers. Unlike you, Mister..." sneaking a peek at Steve's name-tag, "ah, Mister Jefferson Cooper, and may I call you Jeff?"

"If I can call you Krishna," smiled Steve. "I had the luxury of free time this afternoon, so to while it away, I bathed." He forked a long thin slice of run-of-the-mill, dill-sprinkled gravlax-salmon and twirled it round like it was a noodle to fit it into his mouth. He chewed it without pleasure. "There is no flavour in this food. Were it not for your annoying jasmines it would have no smell of any kind."

"What is really annoying is that even though we are in the belly of India's capital, right next door to Connaught Circle, there is not a shred of our cuisine on this table. There never is at this hotel: they like to pretend they are based in some American suburban mall, and sadly the regulars like it that way. They think it elevates them into global citizens, when it actually exposes them for the fakers and parvenues that they really are."

"Are you a businessman, Krishna?"

"Of course. Aren't we all?"

"Some of us more than others. I just tinker, myself. It gives me the excuse I need to attend parties where the most worthwhile smell comes from a bloom that can only function in the dark."

"Well said," beamed Krishna and seemed to be about to heartily slap Steve on the back. Instead, he took him by the arm to steer him to the bar. "Indian cuisine is all about smells. Perfumes, odours, flavours. We will not deem it food if it doesn't blend and marry at least ten distinctive spices per dish. But they have to be the right combinations of spices used exactingly with each other to complement the main ingredients. And of course, used expertly. Never just thrown into a sauce. Sauteed in fat first, to wake up the spices, to help them release their volatile oils to mantle the sauce with magic to drive one mad with desire."

"I've spent much time in India, but I have yet to experience what you're describing."

"Then you must allow me to invite you for a meal. Do you ever come to Bombay?"

"Often. I stay at the Yacht Club. Except when it's under siege."

"I drink at the Yacht Club."

"What brings you to Delhi? Anything you care to share?"

"What are you after in India?" asked Krishna. "Do you really expect to make money in this greedy country?" He smiled bitterly as he handed Steve a tall frosty glass of gin and tonic. "Highly recommended for both Delhi-belly and malaria, to both of which we are subject in this burg despite all the efforts to cleanse it, both of garbage and the homeless, not that I would expect you to have noticed."

"How do you cleanse a place of the homeless? With a hose?" joked Steve, even though his innermost fear was that he would one day end up on the streets and get wiped out during some kind of roundup.

"You ship them off to Bombay. We are a welcoming city. Not at all like Delhi." Krishna took another sip of his drink and deftly put down his glass on the floating tray of an itinerant server. "I'm going to bed," he announced. "You're the only person here worth knowing, but I'd rather continue talking to you on my own 'turf,' so to speak, at my dining room, as your host, a situation where I'm less likely to spill any secrets while I open for you a world of Indian cuisine that can only be found in private homes."

Krishna gave Steve his card with a quick "Call me next time in Bombay," and walked away. Steve waited until he was clear of the doors and headed out as well, to rest for his flight, hopefully to dream of primroses and jasmine instead of shrapnel.

CHAPTER TWENTY-TWO

Varsha met him at the airport in an exaggerated limousine, the kind favoured by dope dealers in New York, complete with divider between chauffeur and passengers. The driver had fetched Steve at the gate and walked him to the car. Varsha was sitting back smoking a cigarette on a long holder, Felliniesque in a stiletto-tight, black two-piece with slitted skirt and a diaphanous mini-bustier that propped her bare breasts to the forefront–just short of the nipples–like a pair of ripe melons framed by the black "v" of the fitted jacket. A flopping felt hat, high heels, thick sunglasses and elbow-length kid gloves–in pink–completed the illusion.

The door had barely been shut behind him, when Steve lunged for her, burying his face in the melons, moaning like a starving child. She stroked the back of his head tenderly, putting away the cigarette, taking off glasses and hat and clicking a button of the control panel at her armrest, in a fluid sequence. The click had activated well-oiled gears that slowly stretched the seat into a flat bed, on which she could return his embrace.

She raised his head from her breasts and kissed his mouth. "I've missed you terribly," she said moaning in her turn. "I've yearned for this moment. It's been an eternity," he countered. He peeled off her gloves and kissed her hands. She undid all of his crucial buttons, belt buckle, zipper. He slid open the clasp of her jacket and reveled at the amplitude barely contained by the bustier. He reached behind her and found the zipper that held the skirt in place. He rolled the skirt free of her hips, breathing deeply of the female essence that was now being freed to mingle with *Opium,* her chosen perfume for the occasion. "You must promise to be mine and only mine," she teased as she closed her eyes, kissed his lips and slid her hand into his shorts. "I am all yours," he whispered hoarsely, lowering her undies. He caressed her delicately in circular tentative feathery titillations that promised insistent tumescence the moment she was primed to it. She nibbled on his nipples, as he drew her closer. He entered her benignly, softly, engaging her in the time-honoured dance and its primordial rhythm, increasing the tempo incrementally, delaying the urgency, setting a fire to heighten desire.

They had mutual climaxes twice in quick succession. Just outside Sultan Ahmet as the Hagia Sophia magisterially poked the sky with her added minarets, and quickly again in Eminönü in tune with a ferry announcing its imminent departure for Kadiköy with several bursts of its horn. Satiated for the moment, they managed to rearrange their clothing, revert the seat back to the upright position, uncork the champagne sticking out of an ice-bucket and pour themselves a drink by the time they had arrived at her apartment building in Taksim.

She lived in a "heritage" building, whose original frontage on Istiklal Caddesi had been converted into a cavernous, medium-priced shoe-store. They entered through the alleyway in the back, now the only access to the prized apartments on the upper-floors, with working fireplaces, fifteen-foot ceilings, original moldings on the metopes of faux-columns that separated the spacious, six-sided rooms, and around the frames of windows that looked out unobstructed into the benign chaos of the walking-street below; beyond into the breadth of the city that descended hurly-burly to the shores of the sparkling Bosporus; hazily across the rushing waters onto the Anatolian shore with its greenery and its mosque-focused suburban villages.

Varsha pointed Steve to the bar and excused herself wordlessly to shower and change. She emerged minutes later, smelling like an English rose, cool and casual in a breezy cream-coloured sari.

She sat on the sofa with an arm outstretched, as if ready to receive the penitent. Steve brought her a frosty glass of fresh pomegranate juice laced with Samos sweet-wine. He tried to excuse himself into the bathroom, but she stopped him with a finger motion.

"No time, my love. A guest is on his way."

"But, I smell."

"Of sex and sweat. Constantine will love it."

"Constantine?"

"My closest friend and most trusted adviser. He's coming to gauge your suitability."

"What should I do to pass?"

"Listen to him talk without interrupting."

Constantine arrived unfashionably on time. In his sixties, with thinning hair but majestically full beard, robust and well-lived, his presence filled the room. He smelled of the many *rakis* that had accompanied his piscine lunch at Arnavutköy Balikcisi, one of the few Istanbul fish restaurants to sell *kalkan*-fish by the piece instead of the entire five-kilo specimen. Instead of a hello he embarked on his favourite tirade against all restaurateurs who couldn't see their way to selling the costly beast by the portion so that he could afford it. He settled on the other end of the sofa from Varsha and examined Steve wearily.

"So, Mister Cooper, you are the new flame in the life of my beloved Varsha. I sincerely hope you are worthy of her, otherwise I'll slice you like a *kalkan* and fry you to a crisp."

"As long as you make them pay for my entirety. I'd hate to be sold cheaply by the piece," joked Steve, refusing to be intimidated by his bulk, his beard, his drunken, bellicose voice.

"We'll see about that when the time comes," said Constantine dismissively. "I have some things to say to you, but I feel like doing it in Spanish. You do speak the language of Cervantes, I hope."

"*Si, entiendo Espagnol,*" answered Steve, appreciating that this was but a ruse at one-upmanship from someone who spoke perfectly good English.

"*Bueno,*" snapped Constantine and continued in rapid-fire if somewhat badly pronounced Spanish. "I know men like you. Roaming the earth looking for bargains, trying to make another million. Well, don't bother. This chocolate box is empty! I know, because I have been here for as long as anyone can remember. I am a Greek with roots that go back to Pericles. We have had the glory and we have suffered the shame, and frankly it is all the same. Bad follows good, doesn't it? It is the law of nature, but once it sets in, it just gets bigger and more excruciating until it makes you want to burst. Our misfortune is bursting like painful fistulas of pus, but the marauders are still upon us. We are but carrion for buzzards and parasites of all denominations. Greece is about to embark on the most fragile economic situation of her long history. The Greek problem has not yet affected us here in Istanbul, but it will, as it will infect the entire world. It seems like a local problem caused by the unconscionable greed of our corrupt, typically Greek politicians and their awful friends, but it is symptomatic of a worldwide epidemic, a disease that will engulf the common person and reverse personal freedoms that have been earned over many centuries at an immeasurable cost of human life." He paused to take a sip of the watered *raki* that Varsha had placed beside him. "It is everyone's fault. We are complicit and accountable in fostering a system, and a hierarchy, and a blind faith in rampant capitalism. We measure success by excess. 'You can't be too rich' say the monsters we have ourselves created, without realizing that only a fraction of us can possibly even remain solvent, let alone get rich. Yes, all of us are to blame, but we don't give a damn because there is nothing new. It happened when the Romans invaded us and bled us dry; same with the Byzantines, just another shade of Roman; again with the Ottomans in the fifteenth century; our own Rich and Powerful after Independence in 1821; the Nazis during the World War; the Allies who drove us into our graves and 'saved' us from Communism by slaughtering half of our people in the aftermath of that war; the Eurozone with their promises of equality as they bought out all our best land to build their repulsive hotels; and the same European manipulators who lent us all kinds of money knowing full well that it would be stolen and misused by the sticky fingers of their counterparts inside our shores, and that they could then confiscate our entire country because we will have to default on our debts; and who knows what horrors that lie semi-awake awaiting their chance to spring out of hiding and maul our exhausted hides, tear out our hearts, feast on our livers, gnaw at out bones. I have a feeling that you are but another just like them, licking your chops in the wings until it is time for the kill, the *golpe de gracia* that will vaporize the final crumbs of our culture and spill whatever remains of our blood so that you can make yet some more bucks."

Steve was taken aback. He ignored Varsha's warning glance and said: "I don't see why you're lecturing me on Greece. I have great sympathy for that delicious little country, which, sadly, I have only managed to visit once. I am not a predator. Just a businessman trying to stay afloat in this messy economy so that I can afford fine presents for Varsha, whom I adore."

Constantine's eyes flashed with pure hate. He continued in English. "Yeah, yeah, you're an innocent little dove! Don't make me puke. You sir, are an unabashed predator. We'll see how much you truly *adore* Varsha as time passes. As for your intentions on Greece, well, you can forget all about them. We will defeat you like we've defeated all your cohorts over the millennia. You see, Greece is the finest place to vacation in all of Europe. This is why your kind has been flocking there, to recharge your batteries and sharpen your teeth, to relax and recoup, so that you can continue ravaging the globe from your head offices in London and Paris and Frankfurt. Greece is ultimately inviolable. Despite our debts and our weak governments and our very own vultures who are ready to tear us apart to feed their greed. Greece will always be propped up, and forgiven all its sins because you need us to continue being just as bucolic and sunny as ever, so that you can use us and milk us for every last drop of our lust for life and our innate knowledge of art and civility. Yes, indeed, we will incinerate all the signed loan-documents, we will refuse to pay back a penny, and then you'll lend us even more money so that we can continue to cook your *souvlakis* and dance the *sirtaki* for your drunken evening amusement, even though you nauseate us and revolt us. We hate the way you look, the way you covet, the way you eat, the stench of your farts, and the stink of your sweat. We laugh at you and deride you, but you still come to us, because you need us. Yes, we will refuse to pay back the money you lent us, and what can you possibly do? Invade us yet again? And conquer what? The awful hotels and ugly holiday villages for which you burnt our forests? But you already own them! Well, go for it. Do it! And to hell with all of you!"

Constantine stood up jerkily and headed out the door with nothing more than a blown kiss to Varsha and a malicious wink at Steve.

"I guess I failed his inspection," sighed Steve unhappily.

"No, you passed," smiled Varsha. "He's a very astute man, especially when he's drunk. He saw through you, he picked out your vulnerability and he attacked you to see how you'd react."

"Did I react well?"

"You almost blew it when you opened your mouth, but he listened to you and responded, which is a very good sign coming from him."

"I need a hug," whispered Steve, curling up like a wanting puppy on the sofa.

"Oh, you need more than a hug," said Varsha throatily. She took many pictures of him and of the two of them together with a small digital camera. "The better to remember you when you disappear again and I have no idea when you'll return," she explained, as she extended a hand to help him stand up and lead him to the bedroom.

CHAPTER TWENTY-THREE

December 8, 2008. This pre-Christmas period was proving to be anything but festive right across the Westernized world, including Singapore, where Steve had already passed the point of desperation. Long-gone the pleasures and the ecstasies of Istanbul and Varsha– even if only just a fortnight old–he was tortured by a disastrous week of continuous losses and devastating reversals.

Tormented by realistic possibilities of being relegated to the terrors of living as broke and helpless as befits someone born in a Texas trailer park, he had sunk into a state of panic. Not a recommended place for a profession that requires the utmost in focus, nerves of steel, and unencumbered patience. He was so upset that he started making fundamental mistakes, not only in trading but also his personal routine, such as arriving at work with his Jefferson Cooper hair and eye-colour, having forgotten to apply the contact lenses and wig, and only noticing his mistake on the elevator up to his office. His secret identity in danger–now even more crucial to maintain than ever–he had exited on his floor and rushed to the emergency stairs, taking them two at a time all the way down forty floors, to sneak out to the street and return to his apartment to correct the mistakes.

His trading was similarly in constant need of corrections and adjustments. His principal account's liquid assets depleted and alloted margins stretched to the limit, he was trading exclusively from the eight-eights which was itself deeply in debt. He was desperately afraid that his creditors would demand repayment and that his nakedness would be exposed. To recoup his losses he was throwing nonexistent money after good, gambling on opportunistic stock, mostly from Istanbul based on rushed and incomplete tips from Hussein, sinking himself ever deeper.

His position became so precarious, and the urgent need for fresh funds so compelling, that he had–with extreme prejudice–no choice but to kiss goodbye to his personal three-point-four million nest-egg that had taken so many-many years of mind-bending work to amass. He looked for a long time at the computer image of his precious little fortune, before he tapped in the transfer information and watched it fly from his clutches into the hungry grip of the eight-eights and then into the void of the principal account. This would give his creditors momentary pause that money was available for them and earn him maybe forty-eight hours of grace.

He was now essentially broke, and would have to work hand-to-mouth, unless he could somehow turn the situation around. The only solace left to him was his cash stash of a hundred and fifteen thousand dollars that his impecunious upbringing had dictated he collect and hide somewhere safe for a rainy day. With the impending blizzard poised to punch him squarely in the face, that money was more than mere solace, it was a dire necessity, even though he was fully aware that were he to reach bottom and get caught escaping with it, they could use it as proof of his criminality and tear him to pieces. Instead of giving in to the terrifying probability of a serious jail term and immediately relinquishing the cash to the Bank, he took it out of its stash, carefully counted it–it was all there–bound the hundred-dollar bills into bundles of ten-thousand dollars, to make them as compact as possible, and immediately went shopping for a suitcase with a false-bottom.

The sacrifice of his three-point-four to the Bank's cause gained him less than twenty-four hours of relief, as payment demands started to rain out of his computer first thing next morning. He placed an emergency call to London.

Within three hours, Mary Tumbril had arrived in Singapore, flown in a special military plane. She was known as *Mary the Terrible,* a name as dreaded as *Macbeth* is in theatrical circles, the mere mention of which was enough to freeze the heart of the most seasoned trader. Her specialty was to uncover skulduggery against the Bank and then unspeakably skewer the perpetrator. Steve, because of his previous successes, was afforded the courtesy of a warning that she was on the way, with enough time to prepare a defense for the red ink on his account. He buried his head in his aching hands and let the impending doom rain on him like icy thumbtacks. He had no defense. Stupidity, counterproductive greed and the inexcusable jeopardy in which he had positioned the Bank were all severally inexcusable. Since all three together had contributed to such enormous losses, they could be deemed indefensible.

He raised his head and took a reassuring look at the view from his window. No, there was no way he was going to give up on any of this. As terrible as this Mary might be, he was smarter than her, and all he needed to do was remain calm and deal with her until she capitulated and authorized more money with which he could trade. It was not going to be easy, but then again what in a life worth living was? He ordered an espresso, loosened his tie a notch and got on the internet to while away the time.

There was a discreet knock exactly at three p.m., the hour she was due to arrive. He got up and opened the door cheerfully. There she was. Thin and little, like a young girl. A trim curvaceous body intentionally voided of sexual allure, rendered unattractive inside a business two-piece, black and severe, with a mid-length slit-less skirt and a long-sleeved, straight-laced jacket; a white satin top with a sapphire-coloured scarf, prissily bowed to one side, its only flourish. Her diminutive face with its fresh skin and pouting lips was framed plainly by tightly stretched hair that culminated in a Dickensian spinster's bun in the back. The mystery of her eyes was hidden behind smoky glasses of a thin perpendicular design that not only cut off contact to her inner thoughts, but clashed with the shape of her face making it seem lopsided and a little ugly.

Steve offered his hand. She looked at it as if it were some suspect object only to be touched with a rubber glove. She left his hand suspended in a grueling fifteen-second wait, until it started to tremble, then squeezed it ever so briefly and raised her eyebrows to just above the rims of the glasses. He stepped aside to let her enter and she passed him with an ice-cold "Please shut the door." By the time he had followed her order and turned around to face her, she had taken his seat behind his desk, where she appeared large, almost formidable, despite her small stature. She had effectively subordinated him into a guest in his own office.

"Please explain to me what the hell is going on," she asked, hostilely focusing her eyes on the wall somewhere above his face.

Steve, uncomfortable in the unfamiliar guest-seat, made a flash decision. His best attack was total surrender. Well, not total: there was quite a large deficit in the error-account, which for now could remain in shadow; but he took full responsibility for the three-hundred million owed by the main account, admitting freely that he had been foolhardy, taking unnecessary risks in the shaky environment that had ruled the market for the past two months.

She peered at him. "It's refreshing to hear you apologize. Very humble. Many are as guilty as you, but none of them would be so forthcoming. However, it doesn't help, does it?"

"No, it doesn't," conceded Steve, lowering his gaze.

"The Bank was among the first financial institutions to be installed in the Royal Exchange, invited by Thomas Gresham himself. In 1568. That would make us four hundred and forty years old. Far too settled to be blown away by a parvenu like yourself. You are about to cause a credit event for us, sir. That would be catastrophic banking news in this chaotic climate. It could bankrupt the Bank.

This is unthinkable. Families who have been depositors with us for centuries deserve better. Do you agree?"

"Yes, I do," answered Steve with sincerity.

"How can I possibly trust you to continue?"

"Trust takes a long time to earn. I have always acted honorably with the Bank. *Trust* is not the issue. But, *continuing* is." She was listening to him intently. Encouraged, he surged ahead: "I am a long-distance runner, ma'am. I'm in this race and I intend to keep competing. I have no choice. The Bank and I both have a lot to lose if I cannot be trusted to continue working out of this office. It would disrupt the Bank's Asian operations; it would weaken shareholder confidence; it would obviate all of my future contributions; and most injurious of all, it would present an impossible conundrum to anyone assigned to replace me. It would be like asking the next person to start trading underwater without scuba gear. That is a formula for guaranteed failure."

"You're the one who sank the ship, Mister Hunter. What could possibly persuade us that you yourself could ever surface again?"

"My indisputable need to do so. This is a matter of life or death for me. If I cannot manage to recoup, I might as well consider an end to everything I have lived and stood for. I know how to do the right thing, and I fully understand the mistakes I have committed. I know that there are 'safe' markets even in the worst environments. Norway, for example. There are no fortunes to be made there, but little gains are much better than big losses, am I right?"

"Anything is better than any size of *loss,* sir. Loss is not part of the lexicon for someone in your position."

"I know," said Steve hoarsely. "I am eager to make amends."

"Well, you're in luck. Everything you have said in your defense more-or-less echoes what we thought as well. We are releasing eight-hundred million pounds to your trading account. We, as you said, should trust you, because you have done well for us in the past, and, despite your recent missteps, you are still the best person to continue for us. However, be warned. I'll be watching you like a hawk. And, if I detect any misconduct, the slightest tendency to be reckless with our money, to make dubious trades, to gamble with the Bank's assets and therefore its very existence, I'll come down on you like a sledgehammer, unleashing all of our might to put you in a jail cell and throw away the key."

"Thank you, ma'am. You won't regret it."

"I hope not," said Mary without a smile. She got up from his chair, and pointed it to him with a sweep of her hand. "Thank you for your time. I must return to London."

"Can I offer you a drink at the Mandarin? They make the best spring rolls in the city."

"You can't afford them," she said, surprising him with a smile. "Hopefully, next time," she prompted as she exited, leaving behind a seductive scent of jasmine and musk.

CHAPTER TWENTY-FOUR

There had been no presents for Steve at Christmas, and there would be no champagne parties for New Year's. On the other hand, there was plenty of desolation and unmistakeable warnings that he was about to vaporize. It had taken him twenty-one days to burn through five hundred of the eight hundred million sterling re-infusion of cash that the Bank had granted him, and now he was irretrievably in trouble.

He had manipulated the money in dubious maneuvers that had crossed the line into crimes, punishable most severely in Singapore where they had been committed. He had tried to keep his promise to Mary Tumbril to take it easy and make safe investments, but his every move was backfiring and conspiring to destroy him. Meanwhile he was abusing the error account to death with barely shielded imaginary transfers of money into it, and trade after disastrous trade from its so-called refuge, hoping not only to cover the Bank's deficits, but also desperately attempting to generate personal profits and rebuild the nest-egg he had had to relinquish. He took no precautions to cover his tracks, to the point that the most cursory audit would conclusively prove that he was cheating *and* gambling, desperate to pull lucky, with no concern whatsoever for the welfare of the Bank. The eight-eights was soon deep in an unscalable hole.

Every seasoned gambler knows that it is useless to chase bad luck, the only sensible policy being to withdraw from the game while still alive and come back another day, fresh and focused. This was not an option for Steve. For all his experience and worldly financial sophistication, he had never been in this position before. He was plagued by the good luck he had enjoyed during his entire career; he had no idea how to retreat. He took shelter in his luck and kept boldly trading on questionable stock, not advisable at the best of conditions, and absolutely life-threatening during a crisis.

On this day, December 29, 2008, a mere forty-eight hours before the end of oh-eight, the most god-awful year since his awful childhood, he was indeed on the brink of annihilation, even though most of his debts were being tolerated because of the fictitious "health" of his main account. Most, but not all. Creditors from the Mumbai exchange had served him notice to repay three hundred million pounds by the close of business on Friday, the second of January. He had two-hundred and ninety-eight million in the main account. He needed two million more to meet the note. He could have just given up at that point, considering he owed an additional eight-hundred million from the eight-eights, whose notes were bound to start coming in at any moment. He was not however ready to surrender. Especially not, because Hussein had forwarded him a supposedly sure thing that should triple in value in the next week. If he paid off Mumbai and remained active, he could reasonably expect to be given the margin to make a giant purchase of the Hussein stock, and bounce back overnight. He didn't even bother to consider how he would be able to defend a major investment on a little-known stock just before its price soared; he would deal with that later. The important thing now was to find two million pounds within the next three days and get back into the game.

Varsha was his obvious answer. In a loose moment, she had bragged to him that she had that much cash in the bank, the safest place she could find for her money, being distrustful of the stock market. He rang Aishe who found him a flight via Bangkok for

Istanbul, departing Singapore at noon and arriving on the shores of the Bosphorus by mid-afternoon. It never once occurred to him that he was on a mission to con his lover out of all her money. In his mind, he would be inviting her to make an investment with which to triple her money in a very few days.

The long flight from Thailand to Istanbul was fully booked and Steve had been lucky to get on it at all, albeit in a middle seat of the *economy* section, squished between two fat people. He was nauseated by the mere smell of the cheapo meal, and he couldn't bring himself to watch films on the tiny screen attached to the back of the seat in front of him. To pass the time and find some recourse from his discomfort, he tried to nap, but that was even worse as nightmarish images sprang up in vivid technicolor the moment he would close his eyes. He saw himself being whipped, being executed, being tortured, and worst of all, living penniless and homeless on the mean streets of an unnamed Texas mega-city. Whereas in the past, nightmares would refresh him on wakening as he realized that he was still very much master of his own fate, now they scared him half to death, since all of their harrowing elements were a whisker from coming true.

He deplaned exhausted and depressed. Not exactly the kind of mood he needed to be in to be able to sweet-talk Varsha into emptying her bank account to him. He needed a providential helping hand and it turned out that Mamon hadn't entirely abandoned him yet: He caught Varsha highly compromised indeed.

He had decided to show up unannounced and finding the building door ajar, he managed to get up to her apartment without being buzzed-in. Varsha answered his ring thinking it was the delivery-boy bringing the kebabs, and froze upon seeing him framed in the doorway. She was wrapped in a large towel, with messy hair and a telling aroma of sweat and stale sperm. She tried to compose herself and try to stop him from entering, but he acted quickly, hugging her and easing her inside the door pushing it shut with the back of his foot.

Constantine, dressed in not much more than his underwear, walked out of the bedroom, strutting like a rooster. "Ah, if it ain't Mr. Jefferson Cooper! And what brings you to us at this most inopportune moment?"

Steve smiled magnanimously, very grateful for this embarrassment. This was exactly what was needed to put her in the worst possible trading position, an easy prey to his proposition. "I missed the great lady, more than she missed me it would appear."

"Varsha is the most eligible woman in this City. Did you really think she could remain an exclusivity of your random visits?"

"Constantine!" shouted Varsha threateningly.

"No, Varsha, he's right," said Steve with equanimity. "I apologize for my presumption, I should have called first."

"Well, I... I... I need a shower," whispered Varsha painfully, "and Constantine was just about to leave," she added meekly as she disappeared into the bathroom.

Constantine shrugged, and leisurely, wordlessly dressed himself with clothes that were strewn all over the living room, as Steve sat back on the sofa with his eyes shut. The doorbell rang again. "Maybe, this time it is the kebabs," declared Constantine as he unlatched the door. He took the packet and paid for it. "Here. The best take-out Turkish burgers in the neighborhood. With my compliments." He put the food down on the table and took his leave without further comment.

Varsha sat down beside Steve, having taken the fastest shower west of the Bosporus. She had thrown on a loose kaftan, wore no make-up, her hair combed straight down with a faint wave at the bottom just north of her shoulders. She smelled of *PeReJa,* the venerable lemon-flower cologne that had once been the favorite after-bath splash of Istanbul's society, rich and poor alike.

She ran her fingers through his hair and cleared her throat to deliver an apology she had been rehearsing for the last several minutes. He hugged her with urgency and pasted his face to hers. He kissed her openmouthed until she started to gasp. He eased her under him as she opened the flaps of her robe. He undid his belt and unzipped his fly and released himself full-force into her womb, deep into her most intimate places. He performed heroically, galloping like a colt and in turn easing into lyrical, flowing ballet-like thrusts. Motivated by revenge for her infidelity and the total submission he required of her for his suspect "business" proposition, he knew that he had to please her beyond any normal expectations. He delayed his orgasm, holding back until he could sense that she too was ready to explode. He kept at it, in pain by now, until he made it happen: a mutual orgasm accompanied by high-decibel moans and total abandon.

Steve kept his dominant position on top of her. He kissed her tenderly. "Is he as good as that?"

She kissed him back and wiggled out of his arms. "I need a cigarette."

Steve rolled off the sofa and quickly disrobed down to his stained underwear. He lit two cigarettes and gave her one. "Is he as good as me?" he repeated.

"Not even close, my darling," she allowed herself a smile. "When he gets excited he farts, and when he settles down, he farts some more. Sometimes he forgets what he's meant to do in-between." She looked into his blue-greys submissively. "He's just a bit of solace for me when my body aches for your touch."

"Please don't apologize anymore," he said dismissively as he sat down close to her, caressing her arm. "It's my fault. I've been too busy making money. I've thought about you, yearned for you... you have no idea."

"I love you, Mister Cooper," she giggled and kissed him. She was in his grasp, ripe for the kill.

He stood up to his full height and took off his shorts the better to dazzle and disarm her for his impending salvo. "I came to you now, not a moment too soon it looks like, not only to love you but also to offer you a very exciting proposition."

"Proposition?"

He sat down close to her again. Her hand, of its own volition, lowered itself to his penis, clutching it as if it were a stick-shift and she was driving down a steep mountain road. "How would you like to quadruple your money in less than a week?"

She was taken aback. Money was the last thing on her mind at this moment. "Who wouldn't?" she muttered amid re-aroused passions.

"This is a once in a lifetime opportunity, but it needs to be grabbed instantly. I flew here on the spur of the moment. It was a full plane, I had to fly economy. I wanted so very much to get to you right away and talk to you in person, persuade you to act, I believe in this so very much; it'll be the best gift I can possibly give you, complete and total independence. Imagine yourself with eight million pounds to your name, instead of only two that you have now. I've been there and I know. Two million can evaporate, eight million is like a fortress–"

"–Two million did you say?"

"That's the buy-in price, yes,"

"But that's all the money I have," she said alarmed.

"Yes, that's true today, but next week you'll be the mistress of eight million," he replied soothingly, not concerned that the most the stock could rise would be two-hundred percent, giving her a potential return of six million in total and not the eight he was bandying now.

Varsha withdrew her hand and sat upright. "I don't know, Jeff. What if it loses? I am happy with my two million. It gives me all the independence I need."

"Wouldn't you like to own a summer home as well as this apartment? And be able to fly anywhere you like first class instead of business? And, buy jewels and artwork without worrying about the cost? And send meaningful presents to people you love? I don't know. Be able to do what an additional six million can grant you?"

"What if it loses?"

"That is out of the question."

"Could I not invest less. Say five hundred thousand?"

She was bargaining. He had her. "No, it has to be the full amount, Varsha. It'll give us the full clout and we'll get a discount on the buy-in." He bluffed; he was on a roll. "Also, this way you are able to match my investment. Listen, darling. I'd take the full amount if it didn't mean selling off assets at great cost. And what really thrills me is that we can triumph together, my beautiful one!"

She hugged him, trembling. "Oh, Jeff...."

He gently pulled out of her embrace, standing up to get another cigarette. "If you're reticent, forget it. You know what they say: *you can lead a horse to water...."*

"And what if we lose?" she repeated.

"Not a chance. Would I endanger so much of my own money if I wasn't sure?"

"But what if you're wrong? There are major problems in the marketplace."

"A bad time is often the best time to invest."

"I'm afraid, Jeff. I am a woman. I have no skills. If I were to lose my money, I'd be lost."

"Ah, but you have me," said Steve. "In the highly unlikely event that this deal backfired, I'd still have some five million pounds worth of assets, and I'd take care of you."

She had run out of arguments. There he was in all his naked glory with a penis at half mast that she knew she could re-arouse on the spot. She acquiesced. She gave him the particulars and the access code to her account and led him to her computer. She retired to the kitchen with the kebabs to warm them up and make tea to wash down her fears, while he did his dirty work.

It took Steve only ninety-seconds to download her money into his main account, completing the three-hundred million he needed to pay off Mumbai; paying off Mumbai; and finishing his business by investing his reinvigorated margin of three hundred million in the Istanbul stock. He then had time to quickly clean up and dress in a towel before she reappeared with the food, the tea, and her palette of undiminished desire.

CHAPTER TWENTY-FIVE

The Turkish company's rumoured merger fell through by Monday morning and it had to declare insolvency. This reduced the value of its stock to zero and in the process nullified Steve's investment, irretrievably eliminated Varsha's nest-egg and compromised the Bank beyond its ability to recover.

The end came swiftly. By the middle of the afternoon of Friday, *January 2, 2009,* demands were served for the repayment of the entirety of Steve's margins (one-point-one billion pounds sterling) before the close of business in Singapore, some three hours hence. Steve clicked through all the emails again just to punish himself. He then shut down his computer, straightened his tie, picked up his briefcase and left his office for the last time, without bothering to look back. He was licked and he knew it and now was no time for emotions and self-recriminations. Now there were a number of things he needed to do in a hurry to save his ass.

The very top of his list was a phone call to his lawyer, Joe Schwartz. There were arrangements in place for an eventuality of just this type, and he followed the procedure that the "careful-to-the-point-of-paranoia" Joe had imposed: Steve went to an anonymous cafe and retrieved the never-used and untraceable cell phone from his briefcase. He dialed a special number that corresponded to a similar phone in Joe's possession.

"How bad is it?" asked Joe impatiently. He knew that a ring on this phone meant great trouble for his client.

"Very," said Steve steadily, while sipping his cappuccino.

"Wait right where you are," instructed Joe and rang off. Steve could sense what Joe would be doing next: Using his other limited-use cell-phone, he would place a call to his connection in the

Justice Department, and hear just how astonishing the news was, without flinching.

Joe rang Steve back to apprise him. "Congratulations, you managed to bankrupt the Bank. It's almost impossible to believe that they recently entrusted you with eight hundred mil they didn't really have, and now with more than one billion in notes that were served in London as well as to you here, they are helpless. They cannot meet their obligations and they are preparing to go under. The news will be released later today at the close of business in London, and the prosecutors both here and in the UK, in neither of which places does justice ever sleep, will immediately issue warrants for your arrest. The Singaporean warrant needs a judge's signature which will be obtained tomorrow morning at eight. After that moment, you will be in grave danger. You know what happens to embezzlers in this town. You must get on a plane before that, preferably under a fake name, *if* you've been prudent and possess such a thing. Now get going. And ditch this phone safely right away. This conversation never occurred. Good luck."

Before throwing the phone into a gutter, Steve placed a call to Aishe to arrange for a flight to Istanbul for Jefferson Cooper, departing Singapore at six next morning; first-class, please. He returned to his apartment and continued his preparations.

He removed wig, contact lenses and padded vest and threw them into the incinerator along with all Steve-Hunter documents in his wallet. He replaced them with credit card and driving license issued to his alias. He retrieved the suitcase with the false bottom, and propped it open to take out fifteen thousand dollars from his cash-stash, of which he stuffed as much as he could into his wallet, hiding the rest in an inside pocket of the jacket that he intended to wear on the trip. He stuck his Jefferson Cooper passport into the same pocket. He packed as many of his more modern self's clothes as the suitcase would hold. He checked three more times that his passport, documents and cash were in the wallet and the jacket pocket where he had put them minutes ago. For good measure he propped open the false bottom of the suitcase to ascertain that the remaining hundred-thousand dollars were still there—as if anyone could have possibly taken them.

Finally ready, he wearily walked to the door from which he could still see his priceless view of old Singapore engulfed in the new. He opened the door and felt some tears roll down his cheeks. He wiped them off with the back of his hand and stepped out of his real life definitively.

Suitcase in hand, he walked briskly down eight floors of stairs to avoid being seen by anyone in the elevator. He snuck out of a side door to the street and hailed a cab. He checked into a small hotel that he had used before as J. Cooper, for the excruciating wait for his airplane. He was hungry and would have dearly loved some of the Mandarin's spring rolls, but he didn't dare. He ordered inferior noodles from the hotel's dining room and ate them, watching doctored news from the island nation's strictly controlled television.

He dozed off, the TV on, into a deep sleep and woke up with a start an hour later at two-thirty a.m. by the alarm he had pre-arranged with the front desk. He showered and dressed in a hurry, checking his pockets and wallet for cash and documents yet again. He considered checking the false bottom of his suitcase one more time, but he resisted the obsession and headed to the airport.

He paid for the airfare with the credit card—it would have aroused suspicion to pay in cash, some six-thousand dollars for the first-class window seat that stretches flat for CEO's who need their beauty sleep prior to arrival. He spent two tense hours in the VIP lounge until boarding time, avoiding all eye contact, buried in the pages of the most recent *Vanity Fair,* his preferred reading-fluff for the monumental wasted-time of air-travel post Nine-Eleven.

On board, his anxiety continued until the airplane cleared Singapore airspace. He relaxed visibly after that, ensconced in the kind of luxury he had taken for granted for so long. Premium-seat soft leather, champagne, smoked sturgeon; his real-life predicament felt so distant that he even allowed himself a chuckle over the royal mess inside which he had cornered himself. He felt giddy. He was going down, but at least he was doing it in style. He flattened his seat and lay back. He closed his eyes and settled into a merciful sleep crowned by a dream about his late mother. He hadn't much thought about her in the past, but now that she was smiling at him from his subconscious, he realized how much he missed her. A tormented soul, that accepted her poverty with equanimity and grace, she had died far too young for lack of affordable medical care. Now that it was too late, Steve yearned for one of her hugs and a whiff of her smell, a combination of fried hamburger and permanent b.o. from a lack of a proper shower, sweetened by a liberal dousing of cheap Mexican cologne. In his dream, she held him very close–he could smell her!–and whispered, "Be careful, Stevie. You are my favourite boy, and I'll love you forever."

He cleared customs routinely in Istanbul and was lingering in the duty-free deciding which brand of cigarettes would best suit his lungs for the duration of a couple of cartons, when he noticed them. Two uniformed police were staring at him intently. Irrational, uncontrollable fear gripped Steve. He dropped the cigarettes and rushed to the exit, displaying the kind of guilty behaviour that would have marked him for a quick arrest, were he actually suspected.

Agitated, breathing with difficulty, he climbed into a cab. He hesitated when asked his destination. Varsha's home was out of the question. As was his own time-share or any of his favorite hotels, places where he was known. In his troubled mind, Istanbul, once his refuge of choice, had turned into hostile territory. He instructed the driver to take him to a car-rental company, something locally owned, not a multinational.

He rented a Hyundai, his idea of a car that was least likely to attract attention. He had no choice but to put it on his credit card, something that rattled his mind. He might seem anonymous on the road, but on the computer he was unmistakably Jefferson Cooper, and one degree of separation from Steve Hunter.

He had never driven in Istanbul before, normally circulating by limousine, or at least, taxi. He entered the cauldron of the metropolitan traffic like a toddler that was being forced to run before he could fully walk. It takes years of experience and a steady mind to survive the driving conditions of the City. Steve had neither. He drove by rote trusting his luck, prepared to crash at any moment.

The only part of Turkey he had visited outside the City was the Aegean resort of Bodrum, sort-of due south from the Asian side (at least it was so by airplane). He followed the signs to "Kadiköy," the gateway to Asia, and they lured him onto the snail-paced congestion of a shapely bridge which was designed to afford generous views of both sides of the City during the interminable crossing. Many citizens still crossed the Bosporus by ferryboat, but the upwardly mobile who never went anywhere without their cars insisted on using the bridge. All of them in unison had decided to drive on it this afternoon and sunset came before Steve managed to crawl onto the other side.

Steve had only a cursory familiarity with the lay of the land south of the City, with a rule of thumb being to avoid any road that pointed to Ankara, which was due east. The south-leading highways do a tortuous meander through endless suburbs as they skirt the bulge of the Sea of Marmara which balloons out eastward before it tapers off to the south. It was close to ten p.m. and sleek with rain before Steve finally cleared the last vestige of the great city and reached the trunk road to Izmir, the halfway point to Bodrum.

The benefits of his first-class in-flight snooze long spent, Steve felt the kind of tiredness that makes for an awful driving companion. He struggled gamely to keep his eyes open and the car on the slippery road, while simultaneously fighting off his ongoing sense of impending doom and a new, even more debilitating panic of instant arrest. He was now dreadfully scared, hallucinating fresh dangers around every turn.

His torment continued and became more acute with every kilometre, until, almost despite himself, he drove into Izmir and located the office of the car-rental company. He had convinced himself that the car itself had become his greatest risk, as it identified him and could trap him into *their* clutches. The night supervisor, a young man who was enjoying phone-sex with his girlfriend to pass the time, put penis and phone call "on hold" when he saw Steve drive in clumsily and come very close to mounting the sidewalk as he brought the car to a stop.

Suitcase in hand, eyes darting, voice hoarse, Steve handed the man the car keys and signed the paperwork, stuffing a copy into his pocket. The transaction barely finished, the attendant retrieved his phone—to attend to his girl-friend. Steve automatically assumed that he was calling the police. He turned and rushed out of the office. Once on the street, he broke into a run, suitcase flaying on his side. A taxi came to a stop beside him, looking for the last fare of his shift. Certain that it would drive him straight to the police, Steve waved him off, relieved to see him disappear. He was a couple of blocks from the car-rental office and out of view. Another taxi materialized beside him. He felt he could trust this one. In any case, he was too tired to continue walking, let alone running. He asked the cabbie to take him to a hotel near the central bus terminal.

He paid the cab at the hotel's entrance and waited for him to gain some distance. He slowly walked the fifty metres to the bus station, shivering as if he were in shock. It took all of his diminished strength to buy his ticket for Bodrum, regretfully entrust his suitcase with the false bottom to the "hold" and board the bus. There were a few passengers up front, but the back was empty, this out of season early morning bus to Bodrum not being a priority of travelers. He chose a seat where no one could watch him, and put his head back. Torrents of long overdue tears clouded his vision and rolled down his cheeks. He sobbed as silently as he could for many minutes venting wetly for all his misfortune. The attendant–a specialty of Turkish buses–pretended not to notice that Steve was crying. He offered him a splash of lemon cologne (not *PeReJa*) to refresh him and a paper-cup of tea to soothe him.

The gush of tears, or maybe the cologne and the tea, had cleared Steve's mind of all manner of debris. He felt strangely relieved. It was a welcome feeling. He wanted it to last. He didn't want to fall asleep and waste these precious moments of peace, which he assumed were temporary and could evaporate any moment. He spent the next three hours staring out the window, thinking of nothing, as darkness slowly dissolved into grey, wet daylight.

The bus made a quick toilet stop. Steve washed his face and without giving it much thought he tore up his credit card and car-rental agreement and buried the pieces into the wastebasket, shoving them deep in discarded toilet paper. The bus resumed its journey past jewel-like coves of emerald water–now a metallic grey in the haze–and came to a full-stop in the Bodrum bus-station.

Steve reclaimed his suitcase and walked unsteadily. He felt disoriented and helpless. He approached a taxi driver and asked him in Turkish if he knew of a quiet hotel. "I know just the place for you," said the man and took him ten kilometres up the coast to Bitez village, to a friend's holiday cottages, which, though shut for the winter, would very likely accept him.

By now Steve was barely functional, his mind like a pudding. He was driven to Bitez, shown to a room and left to himself. He fell back onto the sofa, fully clothed, and passed out for the next twenty-four hours.

EPILOGUE

CHAPTER TWENTY-SIX

Aishe drove me from Varkala to the airport for the flight to Mumbai. It was the last time I was to enjoy freedom for the next three years. She passed me off to a policeman as if I were a football. He manacled me with one half of handcuffs whose other half was around his own wrist. At Mumbai I was met with a more serious contingent of the law, two sweaty policemen and a prosecutor (judge?) in a Mayfair suit and Parisian cologne. They took possession of my remaining cash, more than ninety-thousand dollars, and put it in a plastic bag. Through a glass window of the stuffy office I could see Varsha and her sister waiting for the money, scant recompense for two million pounds, but at least something.

The sweat-stinkier of the two policemen attached himself to me with a new set of handcuffs and accompanied me on the airplane to London. The restraint on my hand made it difficult to eat the in-flight meal, which smelled and looked so terrible that I was happy for the inconvenience. I fell asleep, a black sleep of no dreams, no illusions, no hope, only a sweet aroma of unseen rose-gardens that masked the odour of my keeper.

I was formally arrested the moment I set foot in London and taken to a windowless room to wait my day in court. That day never came. The same evening, a dapper man who introduced himself as Her Majesty's chief prosecutor offered me a supper of poached Scottish salmon with new potatoes and watercress, and a piece of paper for me to sign, wherein I admitted my obvious guilt, taking sole responsibility for my wrong-doing, apologizing to the Bank and its depositors for my nefarious dealings and throwing myself to the mercy of Justice. This way I saved the court system the enormous expense of a trial and was granted a "light" sentence of six years in a minimum security facility; out in three if I exhibited good behavior.

The three years passed slowly but not painfully, except to my olfactory organs that were in constant attack by the essence of an unsavory mix of boiled cabbage, fried mystery meat, the various foul smells of too many people in tight quarters and bucketfuls of bleach. I did my best to avoid befriending anyone, even though there were some fairly interesting white-collar criminals in the bunch. Being the most notorious of the lot, I eventually did meet many of them when at the warden's suggestion I gave a weekly course on what *not* to do when working as a trader for a centuries-old bank, punctuating my lectures with detailed stories of what I had done to force the bankruptcy.

Giving the course was part of my "good behaviour," the other being my volunteer work in the kitchen, something that I found very engaging and ultimately useful: I learned how to cook, something I had never had to do before, not as child in Texas, and never once when in University and out in the business world, except for mixing muesli for breakfast. By the time I left prison, I knew all the secrets involved in feeding hundreds of inmates cheaply yet tastily enough to avoid hunger-strikes. I also knew that those who can cook never go hungry.

The trading seminars and my kitchen duties kept my mind off my plight during the days, but at night, in a tiny cell, enveloped in the pervasive prison smell, I survived the ordeal with unabashed fantasies of the good life I had enjoyed during my career, and wild schemes on how to retrieve it after my release. I spent many happily sleepless nights crunching my possibilities, until it dawned on me that my most realistic opportunities rested not in the big cities of the West, but rather in an unassuming place like Bodrum's Bitez. It was where my new life had begun, where I spoke the language and where I was obviously meant to return. I reasoned that the Turks loved to eat and that in such cultures cooks are welcome. I would get a lowly job and parlay that into my own chef-owned restaurant in no time.... With Miryam at my side.... Or, so went my fantasies.

I was sent packing from prison at the height of the English winter, grey and lightly snowing. I was handed one thousand six hundred and forty-two pounds, fifty pence, which worked out to one pound fifty per day that I had spent in the kitchen. Not a princely sum, but very useful when you have nothing. I was also given a small room in a hotel for the next ten days, after which I was told I must leave England, never to return.

I spent my first morning of freedom in the American Embassy's consular section applying for a passport, the prime requisite for my banishment from England. The consul agreed immediately that I was eligible for my travel document–once a citizen...–despite my crime and imprisonment. I thought I sensed a bit of envy on his part when he reviewed my particulars–which American wouldn't want to bankrupt a British bank?–and I had a brand new passport in my real name in three days.

I found a cheap London-Istanbul flight and got myself to Turkey. I took the shuttle from Atatürk airport to the nearest office of Pamukkale, the best bus company for the ride to Bodrum. I traveled overnight down the coast, doused in cologne, sleeping most of the way now that I no longer needed to have nightmares.

I got to the Bodrum bus terminal in the morning. It was sunny and mild, as if winter was a foreign notion in this land. I was directed to the little local bus for Bitez. It left me off in the center of the village that teems with tourists in summer but was now nearly deserted. Ahmet's holiday-village, in one of whose cottages I had woken up that fateful day forlorn and nameless, was still there just to the right of the main street. I walked up to it wondering if I'd be welcomed.

Ahmet must have seen me approaching because he had rushed out to the entrance beaming. He waited until I was near and he lunged for me with a hug and kisses on both cheeks, as if greeting a long-lost friend returning from battle. I think I saw a tear roll down his cheek. He ushered me in and bade me sit down in the garden while he fixed tea. The mandarin trees as well as the pomegranates were in flower, giving off a faint but delicious fragrance. It felt like I had come back to life.

Ahmet joined me bearing a tray with small, hourglass shaped glasses of a scarlet brew beside a fat manila envelope. "Rize tea, from the Black Sea, where my family is from," he boasted. The aroma of the tea formed a curlicue of steam that blended with the perfume of the fruit blooms.

"I am very happy you came back," he sighed. "Now I can finally rest."

"I didn't realize I had made such an impression," I said offhandedly.

"Oh, but you did," he sighed again. "Here, look." He pushed the envelope towards me.

I opened it and stared at a pile of cash. "Did you win the lottery?" I laughed.

"I thought I had," he said sadly. "The money is yours. Take it. Sixteen thousand dollars. It's yours. I thought I could make it mine. But I've had terrible guilt ever since. Terrible. As if all those gangsters in Newark had infected me. I haven't slept well for more than three years. Well, since you were last here."

"I love the money, and I can certainly use it. But what makes it mine?"

"It just is!" he almost shouted. "Don't force me to explain, please! Accept it and make me happy. Okay?"

"Sorry, Ahmet. I have a funny history with money. Explain, or take your money back," I bluffed, curious to know what this was about, even though he would have had to fight me to get it back now that I was clutching it.

"Alright, I'll tell you, but you have to promise not to hate me too much."

"I promise not to hate you at all."

"You came here that morning looking very rough. You didn't show your face all day. At about midnight, I got worried about you and came to knock on your door, to see how you were. The door was unlocked. You hadn't even bothered to lock your door. This worried me more. I came in and saw you passed out on the sofa fully dressed, even shoes. I decided to make you more comfortable. I took off your shoes and I was about to cover you with a blanket, it was cold in the room, I noticed some items on the floor. Things had fallen out of your jacket pocket and your wallet had dropped out of your pants. There was a lot of cash along with your passport that had come from your jacket and yet more cash in the wallet. I was tempted, for God's sake. You can't blame me. So much money. There for the taking. I didn't know you. Who knew you? So I took it. And, the passport. I took everything. But, I wasn't finished taking. When you confided in me that you had the amnesia, I sold your own passport back to you and took even more money for that. Well, you were obviously very rich and wouldn't miss the money. That is what I told myself. Maybe you didn't miss it, I don't know, but it gave me great pain. After you left, I felt very very bad. All this time. I never touched a penny. The whole time since then, I was hoping you'd come back one day and I could return your money to you. And, finally you are back, and now it's all going to be alright. Isn't it? You have sixteen thousand dollars there. Fourteen thousand I found in your pockets and wallet and two thousand that I charged you for the passport. The four thousand for that scoundrel Ali is lost, I'm sorry...." He trailed off.

I took the envelope and put it away out of his reach. "I'm sorry my money gave you such problems," I smiled.

"You will stay, I hope," he said coyly.

"If you want me."

"I'll have to charge you. After today. Today you are my guest."

"How much will it be?" I asked playing his game.

"Not much. It's out of season. Fifty bucks a day," he said with New Jersey nonchalance.

"Make it fifteen. It is out of season, Ahmet."

"Fine, slaughter me. I don't care. I deserve it."

"It's a fair price," I said evenly.

"I'm sorry to ask," he said, "but what are you? What do you do?"

"I'm a cook," I said proudly.

"But, I need a cook! I do a restaurant here in the summer."

"How much will you pay me?"

"Not much, but you get to eat. And a place to sleep."

"At least you're truthful."

"I'm an honest man, Mister Jefferson Cooper."

"Aah," I started, to correct him about my name, but thought better of it. "So am I, Mister Ahmet." We sipped our teas in contentment.

"Now, I think it's time we sealed our beautiful friendship with a little *raki.* Yes?"

"Please," I said perkily. Alcohol would be the best solvent to help me digest all this news.

Ahmet took away the tea-tray and returned quickly to set up the table for *raki* drinking: a ceremonial ritual that depended as much on its strict rules and approved accompaniments as its promise to inebriate mercilessly. Thin tall glasses, called *kadeh,* a jug of water, a bowl of ice-cubes, a plate of feta around nuggets of lime-coloured melon, and the centerpiece, a freshly-opened bottle of the licorice-scented booze.

He poured good measures of the alcohol into the *kades,* "Always *raki* first," he said, "and you fill with water afterwards, the other way around would bruise the *raki.* See how it turns so cleanly milky? Ice cubes?"

"Love ice cubes," I said amused by the ritual.

He handed me my drink and poised his own in the air.

"Come, we must clink glasses, looking each other in the eye. *Serefe,*" he said as we clinked. "To your honour! And now you must have a sip! Go on, it's delicious." I sipped, it was delicious, as he sipped his, eyes locked to mine. "Now eat some melon and some cheese, it'll open your appetite for more *raki,* so we clink again and you take another sip, and so on until the melon, the cheese, and most important, the bottle of *raki* are all finished. It's the Turkish way of welcome, and let me tell you there is no better, more intoxicating welcome in the world than a Turkish welcome."

After several repetitions of snacking, clinking, drinking, the bottle near-finished and the sky darkening to welcome the evening, he got up to go to the toilet. There was a warm buzz in my brain, as if someone was tickling me from the inside.

A thrilling trill filled the air. It was melodious and inviting, insistent, but not demanding; gentle, refined; ever so subtly shy. It seemed to be coming from a rooftop behind the garden. I looked up and saw her. Miryam, also known as Mary Tumbril, was perched on the ledge of the chimney. She was nude. Her long black curly hair waved in the wind emitting diamond-like sparkles. She seemed like a bird in flight settled down for a quick rest.

I shut my eyes. She had to be a mirage, a drunken hallucination. When I reopened them, she was no longer there. Lingering stardust was all that was left.

Jasmine and musk perfumed stardust, with which I must have mantled my fantasy. She was not really there, I was imagining her, just as I had yearned for her for three long years, even though I had known all along that I would never see her again. I did not deserve her.

Shivers went through me. There was a light touch of a very familiar hand on my shoulder. It felt so very much like her hand.

"You waited for me. You found me," I whispered, as she lowered her sweet face to mine and lightly kissed my lips. I held her at arms' length with both hands just to make sure she was real.

"I love you," she whispered back.

Montreal, June 2013

 Byron Ayanoglu is a writer of many hues. Memoirist, travel columnist, cookbook author, film-scenarist, playwright, restaurant reviewer, novelist. He has published the perennial best-selling Thai cookbook *Simply Thai Cooking* (Random House, 1995; reissued by Robert Rose, 1996 and re-released three times); a recent novel *Istanbul to Montréal,* simultaneously published in a Turkish version in Istanbul; a very popular memoir *Crete on the Half Shell* (HarperCollins, 2004; published internationally; optioned for film), and a well-received satirical romance *Love in the Age of Confusion* (DC Books, 2002). Widely traveled, Byron speaks five languages and lives in the Laurentians north of Montreal in the summer and somewhere snow-free in winter.